Prefabulous Days

Peter Dewrance

Dedicated to all those who were brought up on British post-war prefab estates

Prologue

A young mother struggles with a pushchair across frozen rutted mud. The passenger, a toddler, has been rudely awakened. He's not happy, even though he is well wrapped up against the snow and freezing wind. His four-year old brother tries to keep up, hanging gamely on to the lurching pushchair. He's wearing the overcoat mum has adapted from a cast-off, dark blue serge, and the matching woollen balaclava she has knitted for him. This is his birthday treat. February the fourteenth, 1947. Valentine's day. Mum wanted to call him Valentine, but Dad thought that sounded sissy, so he is now called Tom instead. A proper boy's name. Too excited, he begins to skip, only to fall on the ice, sharp as broken glass. Well, I told you, she says. His little brother Charlie howls.

Chapter 1 | Harry and Olive

July 1932 – May 1947

Harry and Edwin Dobson are in Great Yarmouth for the weekend, near where their elder brother James lives. Edwin's new wife Lily has come along too.

Harry is twenty and has never had a girlfriend. He's the youngest of the three brothers. He left school at fourteen, to work full time at his mother's confectioners' shop in Putney High Street, weighing bullseyes and liquorice allsorts into paper bags. When his mother died, he applied for a job as a trainee bus conductor. All his life he has resented not having secondary education, a privilege provided only to his brother Edwin, who has had loads of male friends and a string of girlfriends. Edwin married in 1928, and his wife Lily has adopted the role of Harry's matchmaker, seeking out attractive single girls, much to Harry's embarrassment. To everybody's surprise, Harry has passed his bus conductor training first go, and is now full time.

At the seaside Harry seems less inhibited, and, rather to his own surprise, he soon finds himself chatting to an attractive young lady on the pier. Despite the disparity between her Norfolk accent and his cockney drawl, they have already progressed to the ice-cream booth. Harry doesn't really know how to flirt but Olive seems to know the ropes, so she accepts this odd young fellow as a challenge. Nothing serious, just a lark.

Edwin and Lily have gone off for fish and chips and when they return with Harry's portion, Lily drags her husband away to a bench where they can spy on Harry and his lovely young companion. Lily knows her tactless husband would just love to embarrass Harry, but she's given him the evil eye. For once Edwin has to forego the pleasure of teasing his baby brother. When Lily sees Harry has shared nearly all of his chips, she drags Edwin over to the pier rail. "Cold chips, my oh my, you know how to treat a girl and no mistake. Are you going to introduce us then?"

Blushing, Harry has no choice. "Oh, sorry, this is Olive. We just got chatting. Olive was brought up on a farm near here, but she lives in Ealing now. She's with two of her sisters, just for the weekend. Olive, this is my brother Edwin and my sister-in-law Lily."

Lily smiles. "Nice to meet you Olive. Just here for the day?"

Olive looks her up and down. "Yes, I come up from London to see my family when I can. We just got the morning bus from the village. It stops at all the villages, Norwich to Yarmouth, so we can catch it halfway at Acle."

Edwin just grins: 'Lovely to meet you Olive. How were the chips?'

Back at James' bungalow, Harry assumes that nothing will come of the encounter, but he feels good about it because it's boosted his confidence. Lily feels good too, crediting herself for finding a girlfriend for Harry, which is not really true. Edwin has forgotten all about it. He's more interested in going to the nearest pub.

A week or so later, Olive writes to Harry suggesting they could meet up somewhere up west. Lyons Corner House perhaps?

She doesn't want to seem to be what they call forward, but she's not had much luck meeting people in London. She's made the break from the drudgery of her life on the farm all right, but now she's got a job in London she needs to get out and have some fun. After her father died, leaving the tenancy with her mother, who couldn't cope, she and her elder brother Albert had to bear the brunt of bringing up their younger brother George, and three sisters, as well as keeping the farm going. Their mother is now in a nursing home, and the farm tenancy is up for grabs. Now she and Albert are trying to get jobs in London for the rest of the family. The last thing they need is to go back to the farm.

Harry agrees to meet Olive the following weekend, just for the day, and a few weeks later they both stay with Lily and Edwin in their terraced house in Tooting. They all get along fine, going up west for the day.

Olive now works as a live-in maid to a Mrs Byrne, the wife of a barrister who lives in Ealing Broadway. A condition of her employment, like all young women in service, is that she cannot receive male visitors, but once Olive has worked a for over a year Mrs Byrne allows her to meet Harry off the premises on her days off, as they are now engaged. Even later, Harry is invited to tea at the big house, when Mr Byrne is away on business. Or at least that was what he said. Mrs Byrne approves of the match, but she's not in a hurry to lose Olive.

Albert is now an apprentice electrical engineer at the Gramophone Company in Maiden Lane, Covent Garden. Neither of them earns much, but they try hard to visit their mother in Acle whenever they can. Harry sometimes comes with them.

Their wedding is duly held in St Edmund's Church in Acle on a bright spring day in 1935. It's a quiet affair, attended by Edwin and Lily, his elder brother James, all of Olive's sisters and her brothers Albert and George. The reception is held at the Church Hall, and the happy couple escape to spend their two-day honeymoon at the Maids Head in Norwich. Everyone has chipped in to meet the costs.

Olive's choice of husband is a mystery to her family and friends in Acle. For years she had been courted by Terry, a handsome and popular local lad who still drives a lorry for his living. For everyone in this sleepy village, their eventual marriage had been a foregone conclusion. Olive likes Terry well enough, and she has kept him dangling for years. Her sudden marriage to this slim shy cockney doesn't go down too well in Acle. They blame the wickedness that is London.

Back in the capital, Olive and Harry set up home in two rooms in Paddington. Now she is married, Olive has to leave her job, but Mrs Byrne pulls some posh strings to find her a job in a custard powder factory, where she rapidly progresses to supervisor status. Even then they can barely afford the rent, so they live hand-to-mouth on their combined wages. Gradually things get better. They even manage a week's holiday in a house on the Thames in 1938, but their dreams are dealt a cruel blow at the outbreak of war. Harry is called up. Edwin and Lily are relatively well off, having bought a house in the suburbs with their inheritances.

Once Harry is mobilised in the RAF, the custard powder factory is closed down and she is redeployed to make shell cases for the front line. She hates her work, and the biological clock is ticking. She has always wanted to have children. She comes up with the idea of pooling resources with her sisters and they all move into a larger rented house in Willesden. One of her sisters now works for a photographic company who supply the reconnaissance wing of the RAF, and the youngest is called up in 1942 to serve in the Women's Royal Air Force, much to her surprise and disgust. It can't have been too bad though, as she meets and later marries the love of her life when she's posted to an RAF station in a place called Stenigot in Lincolnshire.

Olive and her sisters manage to survive the blitz, V1 and V2 rocket strikes and rationing. Occasionally Harry comes home on leave and Olive becomes pregnant with her son Tom in 1943, and again in 1944 with Charlie. At the end of the war Harry, physically unscathed, goes back on the buses and tries his best to bond with these two little strangers who don't recognise him at first and who constantly demand Olive's attention. He rarely talks about his war, but occasionally, after a few glasses of pale ale he reminisces about a family in France, where he was billeted after D-Day. He finds it difficult to live with Olive's sisters and their husbands. In 1947 the Dobson family move out of the overcrowded Willesden house, into a brand-new all-electric, all mod-cons, prefab, kindly provided by Mr Churchill. No. 35 Friars Walk, London NW 13.

Chapter 2 | In the beginning

Transcript: Episode 1 of a series of podcasts recorded during the third Covid-19 lockdown, 2021. Written and read by Tom Dobson.

This is the first of thirteen episodes in a series of podcasts about life on a post war prefab estate near London. The podcasts are based on lectures I have recently delivered to students at the University of The Third Age in Lincolnshire.

1943 -1947

I have a problem recalling whether I had a shower yesterday, but I can remember things that happened even before we went to live in a prefab after the war. I find it hard to tell what are real memories and what are stories others have told me later on, so this is bound to be a mixture of what I think I remember and what others thought they remembered, as well as what I have read in books and found on the internet since. I have been encouraged by some wonderful M3A students to tell my tale, so here goes.

My first memory is just an image. Two little girls, smiling at me through some sort of net. Years later I found out that the girls were probably two cousins, when I was still in a cot. This probably happened when one of my mum's sisters looked after me in the country, when mum was pregnant with my brother Charlie during the war when my dad was away overseas. That's all, just a fleeting snapshot, still vivid in my brain to this day.

At that time, we lived in a rented house in Willesden, along with two aunts and uncles and my cousin Julie. Later on her sister Jane was born there too. I can remember holding the baby. I do remember that house quite well. It was on a hill, and we played with the snails who lived on the steps that ran down to the road, me, Charlie and Julie. We got told off for that too. I also remember the huge billiard table in our front room where my uncles used to play. They sometimes had their friends in. I remember men in uniforms quite a lot, smoking, drinking, laughing. My mum told me later she was always embarrassed when she took me out in the pushchair, because every time I saw a man in uniform I said 'dada'. I have often wondered if she secretly liked that.

Another memory I have of life in Willesden is bath time, when we used to get washed in the tin bath in front of the fire. Think I'm kidding? I remember the water was heated on the kitchen stove, kettle by kettle, to be added to the cold water until it was the right temperature for kids to be washed in. The temperature gauge was mum's elbow. I remember too the thrill of not getting scalded as fresh hot water was poured into the tub. Mum has told me this happened a once a week. She also remembers the bathroom in the posh house where she used to be in service in Ealing sometime in the thirties. It had a built-in free-standing bath sporting claw feet and huge brass taps.

All that changed when we moved into the prefab. To clarify, I'm talking about prefabricated houses, built in sections in a factory, then stuck together in a street, like giant Lego. They were Churchill's answer to the housing crisis at the end of the war. I think we qualified for a prefab because my dad was a returning serviceman, and we were now classified as overcrowded in the house in Willesden. Three families living in a house built for one. The prefabs were a godsend for families like us - they came in sections on lorries to be assembled ready to live in almost straight away. Normal houses took too long to build.

Prefabulous Days

We moved in in early 1947, but I don't remember that day at all. I do remember mum taking me and Charlie months before, to see where our prefab was going to be because it was still in bits in the factory. I do have some fleeting memories of that trip, and they have been augmented by my mother over the years.

We were on a bus, trying to see out of the dirty windows. The prefab site was a good few miles from where we lived, and it was being built on farmland. Something to do with green belt. We should have moved in sooner, but the estate could not be completed in 1946 because of the very cold weather we had that terrible winter. I do remember it was snowing, and Mum said the bus had to go slow because the roads were icy. Even inside the bus we were cold.

I remember catching brief glimpses of snow on fields, stark leafless trees. Charlie was asleep on the bus. Apparently, I was excited and fidgety, which must have been embarrassing for my mum, I suppose, but according to her we were the only ones on the bus by the time it got to the site. When we got off Charlie woke up. The driver shouted, 'Here we are Olive, best of luck'. Charlie started crying when he was bundled into his pushchair on the frozen pavement. I was hopping about, making matters worse.

I already knew that the new house was called a prefab, but maybe I had not understood that it not been built yet. We headed for a barrier in a high fence - one of those you can see through. I remember seeing lorries and cranes on the other side. Mum went up to the barrier and a man in a uniform came out of a hut. She showed him a piece of folded paper she had shown me on the bus, called a pass. The soldier smiled, saluted, opened the barrier and beckoned us in. Then, map in hand, he helped us over the frozen mud to where number 35 was going to be. Then I fell over and cut my knee on a frozen tyre rut. There was no road, just piles of bricks, dotted about.

I saw lorries further up the hill – the estate was to be built on a slope – and other men in uniforms making low brick walls and pouring something into the ground from a machine that went round and round. Concrete. I can't remember what Charlie was doing, but he doesn't remember any of this anyway. He was only two after all. Mum tied a hanky round my bleeding knee and the soldier, who was called Arthur, took us back to his hut and put some proper plaster on the wound, fished out of a metal box with a green cross on it. He said we could wait in his hut till the next bus back was due. Mum asked who the men were doing all the work and he said they were German POWS. Prisoners of war. 'Oh,' she said.

I suppose until then she had never seen a real-life German. Fortunately, I must have grown out of saying 'Dada' to all men in uniforms.

I suppose when you are a child, you just adapt to change. Better than adults, for sure. For my parents, the prefab was a revelation. I now know that various companies made prefabs after the war, and our one was a type called Airoh, made by the Bristol Aeroplane Company. All kinds of materials were used by different manufacturers, but ours was mainly aluminium. Apparently, Bristol still had stocks of aluminium left over from making planes like the Beaufighter, so it made sense. In some ways aluminium was quite suitable for temporary house building – at least it didn't rust, like corrugated iron. But of course it was always relatively expensive, so aluminium prefabs were a one-off really. As it turned out we were really lucky. The Airoh is now regarded as the Rolls Royce of prefabs.

Prefabulous Days

My main memory of the early days was my parents' sense of wonder at it all. Mum was, frankly, scared stiff, mainly because of the kitchen and the bathroom. I suppose the other rooms were pretty much like any rooms in any small house. I remember novelties like the interior window between the kitchen and the living room, or the mysterious electric switch in the bathroom, which turned out to be connected to something called an immersion heater, for the running hot water. This became an object to be revered and feared, set high on the wall, out of bounds to us kids. Revered because of its function, feared because of its reputation of costing a fortune.

The prefab kitchen was fitted out with a row of appliances, all in line on one side, opposite the side door. My Mum was very anxious about the electric cooker, in particular. I think it was a Belling. She had always cooked on gas, so she must have been wary. She reckoned she got electric shocks every time she used the overhead grill. She may have been right about that. The oven was a mystery too, controlled by temperature rather than gas mark, which made her recipes difficult to interpret. Instead of gas rings there were round plates which heated up, but it took ages to boil water. They also stayed hot for ages and she often used to burn herself.

I recall that as well as the cooker, sink and work surface, there was a mysterious gap when we first moved in. Rumour had it that it was waiting to be filled by a refrigerator, something only seen in American films and perhaps in the homes of rich English people. The rumour was true, and when the fridges arrived one day and installed, they were indeed American models called Frigidaire. To me it looked as if a small bus had come through the wall. Beautiful with the domed door, and we marvelled at the light which came on when you opened it. Or was it really on all the time?

The bathroom itself also included a toilet. I really don't know where the toilet was in the old house, but it was probably outside, at the back. Probably best forgotten anyway. My dad was an expert in toilets, it's what he did in the war, and I remember the lecture he gave us on how it worked. For him, the toilet had a secondary function. He used the bathroom rather like a private study, reading the newspaper and smoking his pipe. This memory is olfactory rather than visual, as the smell of pipe smoke and farts mingled gently together and lingered in the hall when he came out.

Chapter 3 | No way back

May 1947

It's been quite a day. All their worldly goods are now safely delivered to number 35 Friars Walk. A strange new home, guaranteed for ten years, thanks to Mr Churchill.

Harry is relieved the move has gone without a hitch. He wouldn't care to admit it, but he's delighted that at last they have escaped from the madhouse they have endured for so long, and above all, their greedy landlord, the aptly named Mr Hardcastle.

The boys are asleep at last, on their mattress on the floor. Something of a novelty.

Olive has managed to rustle up baked beans on toast, despite her fear of the electric cooker.

'Here's to us Olive. The show must go on, as Old Dobbo might have said, never one to scorn a cliché.'

'Well, yes. It's too late now to get to grips with that fire, and we haven't got our bed up yet. Good job it's not too cold.'

'I thought Tom would never go to sleep. He gets so worked up. Not like Charlie, he'd sleep through an earthquake. Do you think we should work out a plan for tomorrow, getting everything unpacked and that?'

'Let's just get our bed linen out so we can sleep on the mattress. I think we should just get some sleep.'

'All right. You get to bed, and I'll do a plan of action for tomorrow. I won't sleep if I don't have a plan.'

An hour or so later, Harry has worked out as much as he can. Prefab Action Plan completed. He feeds another florin into the electric meter, then fills the kettle for the morning and has another look at the mysterious coal-fired stove in the front room. It's all so strange, this compact detached house made of metal.

There's an unfamiliar smell, or perhaps it's just the absence of the smell of the old place, with its stale combination of damp, cigarette smoke and cooking. It sounds different too. Instead of the babble of Olive's sisters and their families, and the background soundtrack of passing traffic and the nearby railway yards, all he can hear is the faint breeze in the tall trees behind the estate, not far from their back fence. No curtains yet, so as night falls he can see neighbouring windows lighting up. In the children's bedroom he spots someone else framed in the rear window of the prefab behind them. Silhouettes, a woman standing next to a little girl. The girl waves, and Harry waves back. The woman joins in. They have no curtains either.

A fleeting moment, a silent film sequence. Up to now he hasn't given any thought to neighbours, but this brief gesture somehow makes him feel better. Maybe this is going to turn out all right after all.

Prefabulous Days

Chapter 4 | Early days

Transcript: Episode 2 of a series of podcasts recorded during the third Covid-19 lockdown, 2021. Written and read by Tom Dobson.

1947 -1955

Our early days in the prefab were spent mostly inside during the winters and outside in our garden in better weather. My dad apparently didn't want us playing in the street, for some reason. My mum had to go along with the ban at first, but she must have talked him out of it at some point, because I remember a few occasions when we were allowed to play in the street when Charlie and I were quite small.

The main attraction was what we all knew as the Green Thing. This was a tall metal object, a bit like a small wardrobe, standing on the pavement close to our side door, much taller than we were. A challenge to the bigger kids who were allowed out, rising majestically out of the paving slabs. My snapshot recollection is playing in a heap of builders' sand right next to the Green Thing.

For a while after we moved in, road work was still going on, tarmacking the roadway, laying paving slabs for the footpaths and adding kerbstones. The labour force was a small gang of detained German prisoners of war, supposedly supervised by British squaddies. Residents were strictly instructed not to fraternise with them, but of course some did, and so did their kids. This was possible because the squaddies seemed to be notable by their absence most of the time, or were otherwise occupied sitting in their hut, drinking, playing cards and smoking. One of the PoWs smuggled toys to us somehow, and I remember with affection the tiny metal tractor that came my way. Or maybe it was a bulldozer. The pile of sand was presumably used officially for laying the paving slabs, but it served well as an unofficial sandpit for us kids. The spoils of war.

I suppose attitudes toward the PoWs must have been divided, some feeling sorry for them, others bitter about them, as representatives of the enemy who had killed our people and thwarted hopes and dreams. Scapegoats. Years later I heard a rumour that at least one lonely young lady felt more than sorry for one of the younger Germans, with consequences you may imagine. Who knows? I have an image in my head of one PoW who smuggled the toy tractor to me, but maybe that image is a figment of my imagination. What I do remember clearly was that the toy triggered a row when my dad found it. As usual it ended in tears. Mine, anyway.

We didn't know what the Green Thing was, neither I suppose did we care. Sometime later I learned it was some kind of electrical junction box. It did hum a bit, as I recall. One of my blog readers remembers it had two locked doors, hinged in the middle, which kids used to use as climbing aids. Sitting on top of it seemed to be the general aim anyway, electricity or not. Recently the true function of the Green Thing has been confirmed by someone who knew – an employee of the local electricity supply company, Eastern Electricity in those days. He states categorically that the Green Thing was indeed an electrical distribution box, known in the trade as a *Feeder Pillar*. He has identified its manufacturer and purpose: 'They (feeder pillars,) came in various sizes and dimensions, and were manufactured by LUCY of Oxford, an electrical castings company still in business today. They were used to sub-divide the distribution of electricity.'

So there you have it, a rational explanation. Rational, but perhaps only of passing interest to many of those who found freedom and power on top of it. I prefer to think it was a prototype Tardis, stranded in time and space, right outside our door, parked up by Doctor You-Know-Who. That would fit with the humming. Well, he was, is and will be a time traveller. No imagination, some people.

What else in those early days? Mondays were always washdays. The one mod-con nobody had then was a washing machine. I can't recall how mum did it, but as I understand it the prefab was equipped with a copper, used to boil our dirty linen. I do remember mum's mangle, which appeared by magic when she lifted the hinged top of the pine kitchen table up. Steaming clothes, fed between the rollers as she cranked the handle, hot rinse water oozing out into a bucket or something down below, mum red-faced and irritable, her glasses steamed up. It seemed to go on all day. I'm not sure what we kids did meanwhile – probably just played in the front room or out in the back garden. When we weren't fighting, we were both happy with dinky toys and a wooden garage my dad made. It wasn't to scale, but we loved it just the same. Dad gave us the choice of colours, and we went for bright red and white.

We had to go out in all weathers, shopping with mum. Because the estate had been built in the middle of nowhere, this meant either walking to and from shops near our school, four miles in all, or catching the bus into town. I remember lugging seven-pound bags home, usually potatoes. Charlie got off light with smaller bags piled on top of him in the pushchair. Of course, dad was usually at work, depending on his shifts. I had only a vague idea of what he did, but I remember he wore a uniform with a peaked cap and sometimes he had a bottle of pale ale with his supper. I had a sip once. It was horrible.

I recall one shopping trip when mum stopped suddenly outside a newsagent shop, transfixed by a notice board on the pavement. The King had died. King George the sixth. Mum seemed upset, and she tried to explain how the King had seen them through the war, and his daughter Elizabeth would now be our queen. We would be the new Elizabethans.

I don't know exactly how old I was when on another day when we got off the bus in town, a strange man came up to us and said something like: 'Hallo Olive, how are you? Is this your boy? How's Harry?' It's mum's reaction I remember most, rather than the man or what exactly he said. She looked shocked, grabbed my hand and we fled down the high street. I think the man laughed. I asked who he was, and mum said never mind him, just some old tramp. I didn't know what that meant. For many years I believed that explanation, but it turned out that he was in fact my only grandfather, our dad's dad.

I had already discovered that other kids had grandparents. Mum told us that Charlie and I had none because they had all died before we were born. Years later I checked the records. Three out of four were dead at that time, but this one was still very much alive. Eventually mum admitted she had lied. To protect us, she said. She explained that dad had nothing to do with his father after he had ditched his family to live with another woman. She added there were children by this other woman, and that they were all bastards. She was half right, there were indeed other children, but quite recently, when I found their grandchildren in America, the bastard bit came as a shock to them. According to them they were born in wedlock, and I have no reason not to believe them.

I digress.

Prefabulous Days

Back at home I began to be aware of our immediate neighbours. Our prefab was at the road end of a row of three, connected by a common footpath. Next door were Mr and Mrs Patterson, Bill and Agnes, and their daughter Mary. To begin with, we didn't have much to do with them, but quite soon mum and Agnes became quite pally, and they used to natter for ages over the flimsy chain-link fence that divided our plots. Often Mary came to play with us. She was about the same age as Charlie, and they were on the same wavelength from the start.

Next to them, in the last prefab in our row, were the Langton family, Mr and Mrs, and their only son Hamish. Mr Langton was a very loud ginger bloke who used to run a lot on the hill behind the estate, with a pack on his back. Always hearty and loud. Dad told me he had been a sergeant in the army. He once showed us these tiny holes in the back of his neck and stuck matchsticks in them. War wounds, he reckoned. Weird.

I don't remember Mrs Langton, but one day all the kids from the neighbouring prefabs were invited to Hamish's birthday party, including Charlie, Mary and me. It didn't last long. Mr Langton showed off with his boring matchstick trick and tried to get us to do PT exercises in their back garden. Right after we had stuffed ourselves on cakes, fizz, and sweets. They had a gramophone and tried to get us all to sing along to some scratchy old record. Something to do with birds singing in a tree. Karaoke before its time. Halfway through the song Mary threw up dramatically into the open stove, the prefab version of central heating, instantly extinguishing the glowing coals amid a cloud of steam and puke-fumes. Hysteria set in. Party over. They were probably afraid that vomiting might be catching. Years later Mary admitted she'd thrown up on purpose. Cock up on the kiddie front, Sergeant.

Hamish himself was a pretty blond boy, the apple of his parents' eyes, supposed to be frail. We were under orders to go easy on him on the rare occasions he was allowed out to play. The Langtons moved out after a boy called Max Flack peed over Hamish's blond curls from the top of the Green Thing. Kids who had been there were graphic in their accounts of this jape. They revelled in the image of green piss seeping down through poor Hamish's lovely locks. It became an estate legend.

Max grew up to be quite a character. Not a great talker though, more of a quiet doer. His mum, according to mine, had no control over him. They lived in the row behind us, where the prefabs had back gardens backing straight on to the woods bordering the hill behind the estate. As a teenager he got the motorbike bug. Their front and back gardens became littered with spare parts, stripped-down frames, oil cans and the like. Occasionally complete rebuilt bikes would emerge, throbbing and gleaming. He used to park the latest model by the Green Thing, with a for-sale sign on it. Mary claims she had a few illicit pillion rides.

Unfortunately, some spoilsport must have complained about the mess, noise and exhaust fumes. Running a business from a prefab was not allowed by the council, and they shut him down. Or so they thought. Not to be beaten, Max just brought it all indoors, tidied up the frontage a bit and converted his bedroom into a workshop. Rumour had it that Mrs Flack had been spotted riding pillion, kitted out with crimson and black leathers, heading North. I have no idea how Max ended up, but if there's any justice, he must be a millionaire by now.

I hope so, if only for his mum's sake.

Chapter 5 | What do we do tomorrow Mum?

September 1947

On his day shift, dad normally gets home at five. Olive always tries to time their tea for six so Harry can change out of his uniform and, hopefully, unwind. The boys are always excited by the time he comes in. In fine weather they are allowed to wait outside, in the front garden, to spot him as he comes into sight after he has walked from the railway station. Sometimes they all go down to the main road to meet him there. This is such a day, Tom's first day at school. In his head Harry is still on his bus, still feeling bad about the woman who had tried to dodge her fare, even though she probably had plenty in her purse. He might have been sacked if he let her get away with it, but a nice old lady had paid for her. All in a day's work, but it still disturbs him.

Olive gives him her usual kiss, but Tom claims his hand. He is bursting with the news. 'My teacher said I did a nice drawing, dad.'

'That's good! What did you draw?'

'Your bus! And you were ringing the bell. I did a drawing of our house as well, with all of us in the garden. I can show you when we get home'.

Charlie just grins, content just to see his dad and push dad's bag along in his battered old pushchair.

Back home, the drawings are displayed and admired in the front room. Tom is on a roll now. 'I tried to draw you giving someone a ticket, but I couldn't fit that into a window, so I thought about what else I could do. You can't really see the bell thing, but I can have another go at that.'

'Hang on, why is there no driver?' says Harry.

'It's not finished. Teacher said I could draw the driver for homework.'

Back in the front room, Harry looks up and watches Olive through the window between the front room and the kitchen, as she attacks the dreaded cooker. One of the many natty features of the prefab, this internal window, which allows Olive to keep an eye on the boys in the living room while she's in the kitchen, and the other way round. Harry reckons no home should be without one. Harry is still curious about Tom's day. He picks up the thread. 'Your teacher, what's her name? Is she nice'?

'Yes. She seems nice, a bit like an auntie. Um, I think it's Mrs Nixon. Or it might be Miss Jones. I'm not sure.'

'So, tell me what else you did.'

'Well, first we were in the playground, then a teacher blew a whistle and we all went with her inside and we sat down in this room with desks and she gave us these things called slates and said we could draw on them with these funny cold pencils. Some of the other kids cried when she went out, but I didn't. One of those boys from up the road said we had to do real writing and he pretended he could do it but he wouldn't let us see his slate thing. He said if we couldn't do real writing, we'd be smacked, but I didn't believe him. I think he was trying to make us cry.'

Olive and Harry exchange a look. A delicious smell of sizzling sausages was floating into the front room. She's getting the hang of that bloody grill now, Harry thought.

'So who's this boy from up the road then?' Asks Olive, shouting over the noise of grilling bangers and boiling greens.

'I don't know his name, but I've seen him on the Green Thing. When the teacher came back she was cross with him because he made some girls cry, and he had to stand in the corner, but he was still laughing. Then we went out to play again and after that we did some more drawing but this time we had some paper and coloured pencils. That's when I did the bus and our house.'

'All that drawing! You must have been tired by then' says Olive.

'Not really, but then we all went out to play again and then we went in this kind of hut for dinner. It was horrible.'

'How was it horrible?' asks Harry.

'It didn't taste nice like mum makes it, and we weren't allowed to talk or make any noise. We had to eat everything too. Or else. The gravy had these lumps in it. The pudding was worst. The custard had lumps in it too. It made me feel a bit sick.'

Another look of parental concern.

'Then the other teacher read a story to us. It was about a crocodile who had toothache and went to the dentist and played hanky-panky because he was frightened. He was very naughty and hid on top of a cupboard. I never heard of hanky-panky. I think he was just scared of the drill. Then it was home time and mum and Charlie were outside to take me home. That naughty boy poked his tongue at us.'

Olive can confirm this crime. 'Yes, I saw that. That is hanky-panky if you ask me. Your tea's nearly ready now, so who's going to set the table for me?'

Charlie runs smiling into the kitchen. He loves helping mum with the cooking. He knows which cutlery to use and how to set the places properly. He's happy to be doing something useful, leaving the gab to his brother. Olive puts their food on the kitchen table. They rarely eat at the dining table in the front room.

'Well I hope you'll like this better than that school stuff' Olive says as they sit down to eat.

After tea, the boys play with their toys and listen to Children's Hour on the wireless. Olive washes up. Charlie and Harry dry.

Olive smiles about something as she rinses the plates in the built-in kitchen sink. Charlie is back in the front room, job done, full marks.

'What's so funny Livvy?'

'Well, it's Tom, it's that way he has, sort of grown up and serious when he talks to us. When he came out the gate, he just said hallo, and no more than that, so I said something like, well how did you like school then? He thought for a moment, the way he does, with his head on one side, then he came out with it. 'It was quite nice mum. What are we doing tomorrow?'

Charlie grins. Harry ponders. The dirty washing up water gurgles down the plughole. The sky darkens over the estate.

'Blimey Olive, who's going to break it to him?'

Chapter 6 | People-Power

Transcript: Episode 3 of a series of podcasts recorded during the third Covid-19 lockdown, 2021. Written and read by Tom Dobson.

1947 - 1953

Soon after we moved in, a tenants' association was formed. As kids we were oblivious of this grown-up stuff, until we heard mum and dad talking about it, usually after a letter or notice was posted through the letterbox. Somehow Charlie had taken on responsibility for picking up the mail and depositing it on the kitchen table. The first outcome I remember was a gardening competition organised by the association. All tenants could join in, and there were various prizes and grades of achievement awarded by judges. Dad was very sceptical about the idea of a tenants' association, and this competition in particular. He took a dim view of people who set themselves up as judges of any kind. Mum was keen though and set to with a will in the front garden, growing flowers around the two small patches of lawn either side of the concrete front path. This was forbidden territory for us – we could only play in the back garden, which was fenced off to protect us from unnamed perils on the street.

Later mum became more adventurous, but as a relative beginner she must have stuck with traditional flowers that were easy to grow. I remember some of them. Ice plants, Nasturtiums, Daisies, Marigolds, Antirrhinums, Sweet William, Lupins, Roses, London Pride. I loved them all and I was fascinated to see them growing and blooming. Charlie wasn't too interested because ball games were banned there. Mum used to go for walks around the estate, spying on other gardens. I suspect she was not alone. The excitement was infectious as judgement day loomed. We were away when it finally arrived, but I can never forget mum's disappointment when we came home to a card on a stick in the lawn bearing only the word 'Commended.' More or less everyone got the same result, with only a few getting 'Highly Commended' and even fewer actually winning awards, first, second and third.

Mum's disappointment turned to anger when she inspected the winning garden. Apparently it was resplendent with gnomes, a miniature windmill with sails that turned in the wind, and the like. (We kids rather liked it.) She and dad suspected undue influence with the judges and the elected officers of the tenants' association, and unspecified dirty dealing. I suspect all they were guilty of was poor taste. We all felt sorry for mum, but I think this event just stiffened her resolve to do better. The real enemy was the soil, categorised as London clay, not improved by copious amounts of buried rubble, generously donated by the builders. Later in life Olive became a doughty and successful gardener, growing vegetables and flowers almost to her dying day, conquering all types of soils and weather. The garden competition was never repeated.

However, despite my parents' reservations, the tenants' association came into their own when they organised the Coronation street party in 1952. Impossible to forget that great day, when all the kids on the estate sat down at all kinds of tables, snaking down Friars Walk, from right outside our place almost to the main road. Union jacks were flown, tables were decked out with all kinds of coronation decorations. Bunting everywhere. We all got a union jack to wave, a coronation mug and a special commemorative pound coin. Collectors' pieces now, I bet.

The achievement was notable as an example of community spirit and triumph over adversity when, with little notice, the council tried to cancel the event because they were scheduled to dig the road up. Dad worried that we could fall into a hole. I can only imagine the dismay caused by the council's decision, but their workmen did indeed dig their holes, only days before the celebrations. Undeterred, the people won the day. Tables were simply arranged between and around the holes, and everyone just ignored them. I remember one kid who, once he had eaten his cupcakes and swallowed his special coronation pop, clambered down in one of holes and came out with a handful of beetles, bent on mischief with girls' blouses.

When the bun-struggle was over, we all lined up on the pavements, for dancing, to be followed by a special surprise treat. This was preceded by an announcement over the loud hailer, and some stirring music. Then a coach turned up and disgorged a bunch of tall black men in shorts who ran about lobbing a rubber ball between themselves. The announcer, now falsetto with excitement, introduced them:

'Welcome the world-famous basketball team, the Harlem Globetrotters!'

Gasps from the mums, confusion among us kids. Applause and whoops among those in the know. The world champion basket-ball players proceeded to put on a show of their amazing athletic skills with the aid of portable baskets on stands, then invited us kids, mums and dads to join in. Charlie went for it, but I hung back, simply overwhelmed by it all. As if that were not enough, more wonderful creatures came bounding out of the coach, lithe black girls in noticeably short skirts, gyrating and chanting, swinging furry balls on the end of strings. Pom poms, mum said. Cheer leaders, Mary said.

Some of the dads were well into their ale by now, trying hard not to show their fascination with the sexy cheer leaders, while many a mum was transfixed by the rippling muscles of the Globetrotters who gave them the eye whenever they could. Finally we all stood for the National Anthem, three cheers for the Queen and the Star-Spangled banner. I bet a few new conceptions were achieved that night as memories of the ghostly athletes and pom pom girls faded away under the electric street lighting.

Looking back, some thoughts strike me about that day. I suppose it was the first time Charlie and I ever saw black people, in the flesh. Maybe kids who had TV sets at home were familiar with the phenomenon, but it was news to us. There were no black kids at school, and if there were black people in the high street where mum shopped, I would have noticed. Nobody told us that four years before, the Empire Windrush had docked at Tilbury from the West Indies.

Another thing. At the party, we only knew a few of the other kids, only those in the prefabs near us. Though the estate was relatively small as council estates went, tribalism must have occurred spontaneously. Even though it was technically one thoroughfare, Friars Walk was not aptly named. It wasn't a way to anywhere. If Friars had once walked it on their way to their abbey, they would never have arrived, because the layout was a kind of circle, with only the one tangential connection to the outside world. If the Friars didn't give it up as a bad job, they would circulate for ever. From any one window or back garden, you could only see a handful of neighbouring prefabs. It was only when my dad relaxed his ban on playing out, that we could have discovered other clumps of prefabs, and found where other kids lived. For the first few years I didn't venture far, unlike Charlie, and my mum's circle of friends was limited to perhaps no more than those who lived on our corner.

Prefabulous Days

These days I sometimes reflect on the concept of community. It's easy to assume that there was a higher degree of social cohesion among the post-war prefab dwellers than I see around in these house-owning days. Perhaps we have romanticised this short-lived period in British history, seeing it now through rose-coloured specs. It's true that mums chatted daily over their skimpy fences, and most kids enjoyed the freedom of the streets, but that still happens on all kinds of housing estates. I'm not so sure about the dads, because ours was, in those early days, not inclined to join in. His social life, if he had one, seemed to be at work, punching tickets on his bus, chatting up passengers and mixing with colleagues.

The post-war popularity of tenants' associations interests me too. It seems that they were essentially a nineteenth century invention, which went on to have their heyday between the two world wars. In the fifties, they proliferated, especially in compact, mainly working-class areas. Post-war prefab estate communities were composed of multiple identical family units, housing strangers flung together in a crisis. The housing problem at the end of the war demanded a quick and elegant solution; in practice it was just a matter of random allocation of families to houses. A lottery with no prizes other than short-term comfort and security. I would like to think that the tenants' associations were spontaneously created by decent, community-minded people who meant well, with a feeling for the common good. But their power waned later when British people became more affluent and individualistic, from the sixties onward. My father's dim view of our association may have been due to his innate lack of sociability, but ironically it could have been prescient.

In 1968, when the prefabs were finally scheduled for demolition, the power of the Friars Walk tenants' association was finally tested, and it failed at the first hurdle. The committee voted not to resist the edict. Harry Dobson and Bill Patterson made a quixotic last-ditch attempt to persuade families to defy the bulldozers, but most of them were easily bought off by the council, who bribed them with the prospect of cosy flats. Appeals to any sense of community spirit must have sounded hollow by then. If it had ever existed beyond friendships between close neighbours, working-class people-power on this estate must have died sometime between the pioneer days of the late forties and the late swinging sixties. Not long, just twenty years.

But at the time, none of that mattered much for us kids, who like children everywhere, simply adapted to our situation, unaware that other children elsewhere lived very different lives. Out of school hours, life for Charlie and me consisted largely of playing with Meccano, Brickplayer, Plasticine and an odd assortment of donated or dad-created toys, watching other kids playing on the Green Thing and going out with mum shopping, helping in small ways around the house, squabbling and navigating the moods of our parents.

Chapter 7 | The optician

1951

'Mum, mum……………..Tom's gone blind. His eyes are all glued up…….'

It's seven o'clock in the morning. Charlie is upset and runs to their mum. Tom is awake but he can't open his eyes because his eyelids are stuck together with a crusty yellow discharge. He's still in bed, hiding under the blankets.

Olive leaves the kitchen and comes into the back bedroom. She's trying not to panic: 'So let's have a look then. Oh dear, looks like you might have an infection. Has this happened before?

Tom sits up, shivering. 'It was like this yesterday, but not so bad – I could see all right'.

'You should have said. I'll get some warm water and cotton wool so we can get those eyelids open. Charlie, you can have your breakfast while I see to Tom.'

'I'm not hungry Mum. Can't I stay with you?'

When Olive has bathed Tom's eyes with some boracic eyewash she has in the medicine cupboard, she sees them off on their two mile walk with the other kids to Friarscroft Primary. When they come home in the afternoon Tom seems fine. The next day, the same thing happens. Olive is really worried now, so she mentions the problem to Harry that evening.

'Probably conjunctivitis. I remember having that when I was a kid. Sounds like you're doing the right thing anyway. Let's see if it clears up on its own. Is Tom upset?'

'No, he seems all right once he gets to school. I asked Agnes what she thought and she said much the same as you. Charlie's a bit upset though.'

It did clear up, but it took longer than they had expected. Sometimes Tom was not his usual cheerful self, and he seemed tired. Then one day he came home with a note from his teacher:

Dear Mrs Dobson,

I am a little concerned about Tom's behaviour in class, so could we have a chat after school one day?

Yours, Annie Walcott.

'Well,' said Mrs Walcott, 'it's just that I have had to tell Tom off for chattering in class several times lately. I know he is a chatty boy, but he isn't usually disruptive in class like this.'

Olive is surprised. 'Disruptive? How do you mean?'

'Some of the other children are a bit upset when he starts whispering when I'm trying to talk to the class and I'm having to discipline him. I have asked him why he's doing this, but all he says is sorry Miss. At first I could not work it out, but then I realised he was also squinting to see the blackboard. And his writing has suddenly gone haywire too. I think he can't see properly. Have you noticed anything like that Mrs Dobson?'

'Now you mention it, I have noticed the funny writing. He did have a bout of conjunctivitis a few weeks ago. Could that be anything to do with it?

'That's interesting, quite a few children here have had that. It's very contagious. I don't know, but I think we should contact our school nurse. Would you agree to that?

'Of course. Do I have to do that?'

'No, I'll phone her and let you know when to come in. Meanwhile I'll tell the headmistress about this and recommend that Tom stays off school until something can be done.'

Olive relates the conversation to Harry. 'Should we have a talk to Tom do you think?'

'Well you know how he gets so upset, but let's have a go.'

Harry and Olive broach the subject at bedtime. To their surprise, Tom doesn't get at all upset, and he seems relieved about being off school. This is unusual, Tom loves going to school. The next day Charlie hands over another note, asking Olive to bring Tom to school to see the school nurse. There seems to be some urgency now.

The nurse tests Tom's eyesight and looks in his eyes with an optical instrument. Her opinion is that Tom's eyes may have been damaged by the infection. Usually such infections clear up naturally without any complications, but sometimes some of the eye muscles can be damaged, so she would like to refer Tom to an ophthalmic specialist. She assures Olive that this will be free, under the NHS.

An appointment is made to attend an eye clinic, which is some miles away, and they have to change buses to get there. The unsmiling Doctor Fenwick is very thorough, carrying out more tests with more complicated instruments. He doesn't go in for bedside manner. Eventually he pulls no punches. He confirms the nurse's fears, then explains that the infection could have been bacterial or viral. If it is bacterial, with luck, he might be able to save Tom's eyesight with a course of a new type of medicine called an antibiotic. This would mean Tom being off school for at least three months, and weekly checks at the clinic. Before they leave, the doctor softens when he sees that Olive is fighting back the tears.

'I'll do my best for Tom you know. These antibiotic drugs are a bit experimental, but I have used them to great effect in the army, with bacterial eye infection. If the dose is right and you stick with the treatment, I think there's a fair chance we can eliminate any further infection. Then we should be able to correct his eyesight with spectacles, though that's going to take time and patience. I'll be writing to you formally, with all the instructions and I'll issue the necessary prescriptions for your local pharmacy as we go along.'

'Thank you, doctor. The school nurse said treatment is free under the NHS?'

'That's quite right Mrs Dobson. It's a wonderful thing. Tom's a lucky boy. Without the NHS this treatment would cost thousands.'

Back home, Harry listens in stunned silence. Olive finally weeps.

Over the following weeks Tom gets used to the thick gooey ointment mum or dad puts in his eyes, and the clinic visits. After a while he and the doctor have interesting conversations, about some of his work in the war, Tom's hobbies, Charlie, Mary next door, even the mysteries of the Green Thing.

Doctor Fenwick, a rather dour figure, seems to enjoy these sessions. 'You have a very bright son there, Mrs Dobson. He'll survive this setback.'

Doctor Fenwick also says Tom's eyesight might be fully corrected over time, but he is never precise about how long it might take. Tom gets used to having drops put into his eyes to dilate the pupils and seeing the world like an overexposed film. When he finally gets his first pair of NHS glasses he can't walk properly because he cannot judge where the ground is. All he can manage is a kind of goose-step. Olive thinks he's mucking about again.

Tom wears his glasses until he is sixteen, but sometimes he gets headaches if he reads too much. During those eight years, his eyesight is tested numerous times, and he has been issued with new glasses nearly every time. He has collected all his glasses and keeps them in a special box.

Though Doctor Fenwick has saved Tom's eyesight, Olive notices a change in her elder son. She thinks he has changed from the cheerful boy he was. She ought to know, as she has spent so much time with him at home before his return to school. He was still talkative and funny when they are alone, but since he's gone back to school, he seems anxious. Olive tries to find out what's wrong, but he just says, 'I'm Ok mum.'

She decides to find out what's really going on, and has a chat with his new teacher, Mr Valentine. He finds out that Tom's classmates have been bullying him. They call him four-eyes or specky, and sometimes they steal his glasses and run off with them.

'It's not surprising Mrs Dobson, but don't worry, it won't happen again.' It doesn't.

Olive and Harry sometimes hear Tom crying himself to sleep at night, and, unlike Charlie, he avoids going out to play, preferring indoor pursuits. Once or twice Charlie has comforted him at bedtime, even cuddling up with him in the narrow single bed until Tom has dropped off. Harry's not too happy about this, but Olive argues that they should not interfere. Mr Valentine has been watching both boys at school. He has noticed that whereas up to now Tom has tried to protect Charlie in the playground, now it's the other way round.

Olive reports back to Harry. 'That man's the best teacher in that school. He knows all the kids like they were his. They all seem to adore him. Tom is always telling me about how he sings with them in class, playing his guitar. Now both our boys want guitars. Anyway, we're lucky with Mr Valentine.'

Tom has also been put down a class, finding himself with younger children, and he doesn't like his new teacher much. He reacts in a way that is to repeat itself until he leaves school. For now, he decides work extra hard to catch up with his year group and prove himself to be as clever as his peers. Six months later he achieves his immediate goal. He's back with his former classmates, but things are somehow not the same. Olive thinks he feels he has to make friends all over again.

Chapter 8 | School days

Transcript: Episode 4 of a series of podcasts recorded during the third Covid-19 lockdown, 2021. Written and read by Tom Dobson.

1947 - 1954

Our prefab estate was about two miles away from the nearest school, Friarscroft Primary. In those days unless you were wealthy enough to go to a private school, you were allocated a place at the nearest state primary school. None of this choice stuff. Friarscroft had infants' classes for children from five to seven, and then you moved up into the junior classes until you took your eleven plus exam, just the same as all primary schools in England. Of course, for us it was just school, a place where you went with other kids every day except Saturday, Sunday and holidays, to learn things from people called teachers, mostly ladies.

I can recall my first day at Friarscroft. I remember playing in the playground, scribbling on a slate with a slate pencil, drawing with coloured pencils. There was a naughty boy too who made all the girls cry and got told off. My mum remembers how I didn't realise that that day was not a one-off. But most of the following days are now a bit of a blur. Who really remembers that stuff? At the end of my primary schooling, I could read, write, do some sums, and play some games, so they must have done something right, I guess.

I don't remember it, but I'm told that for a while there was a special school bus which used to get kids to school and back to the prefab estate every day, along with their mums. I think this was provided thanks to the tenants' association and I have a hazy recollection of this bus, but it cost money, so my mum had no option but to walk with me and my brother instead, at least until we were old enough to make the journey unsupervised. How many five-year old children walk four miles a day today? Or how many mums, come to that?

There are a few fleeting impressions which remain. One was being allocated a desk next to a girl. A girl! I think her name was Hilda. Or was it Elizabeth? She was quite nice really, though she was always chattering to me like I was her brother or something, and she couldn't sit still for long. Fidgety Fiona. This used to get me into trouble with the teacher, probably because I was a chatterbox too. Teachers were stricter in those days. I can remember drawing and painting, which I loved. At breaktime, we all stood in two lines, boys and girls, holding hands, and went to the toilets then washed our hands before we could play in the infants' playground. I think this was just running around like mad things, ball games and for the girls, skipping. Endless skipping.

Three, six, nine, the goose drank wine,
The monkey chewed tobacco on the tram car line.
The line broke, the monkey got choked,
And they all went to heaven in a little rowing boat,
Clap-Clap! Clap-Clap! [Trad.]

We also had to drink milk, which I didn't much like. I hated the smell of it. It took something like forty years to discover that I have an intolerance to cows' milk.

I suppose I had school dinners at lunchtime in the infants. My recollection of them is more to do with the junior school. I don't really want to get into the whole school dinner thing, but just to say that the cooks seemed to specialise in lumps.

Lumpy mashed potatoes
Lumpy gravy too
Warm lumpy custard
Tastes like mustard
Lumpy stew
Just for you. [T. Dobson, 2021]

If it had been possible to produce lumpy cabbage or carrots, they would have served them too. Instead, they were just sodden, mushy and tasteless.

Not only was the food unpleasant, so was the iron discipline meted out by teachers on dinner duty in those days. There was no choice, just the *plat du jour*, repetitive variations on the theme of post-war English stodge. Main course: meat and three veg, typically including mashed potato (with lumps), vegetables boiled to within an inch of destruction, gravy – thin, tasteless. Pudding: typically, jam roly-poly (aka Dead Man's Leg) or Spotted Dog and custard, also with lumps, or a milk pudding such as semolina or rice pudding. They made me feel sick. They still do. Especially rice – all those lumps.

The house rules were made clear from day one: no-talking-and-eat-everything-on-your-plate, or else. Or else what? The soundtrack was a symphony of food splatted on innocent cold plates, knives and forks clattering and the heavy echoing footsteps of the teachers in charge as they patrolled the prefab canteen. Not so far from Mr Bumble's establishment really, but I was no Oliver.

By the time I went up into the Juniors, Charlie and I were trusted to walk to school and back with other kids. Our route used to vary, but it always involved crossing the main road and walking through a residential area and the shopping parade. I remember being bitten by a dog. An Airedale as I recall. I still steer clear of them. And those winter days when my balaclava would freeze to my face and my woollen socks froze to my legs. All school clothes were made of wool then. By order of the Queen. Or maybe the Duke of Edinburgh. On wet days, the smell of wet wool in and outside the classrooms is something you never forget.

When we walked home from Friarscroft, we often passed the home of a gnarled old man who used to invite us into his garden and talk to us about his life. Good job my dad didn't know. This bloke claimed he had spent many years alone, stranded with the natives in the African jungle, and that he was in fact the real Tarzan. I supposed he got lost and couldn't find his way out. The reason he was now living in suburban obscurity was that he had been ripped off by Edgar Rice Burroughs.

Today's parents might like to know we were not abducted in three years of unsupervised walking to school in all kinds of weather, crossing main roads, and chatting to an old man, loony or not. I like to think we were healthier and more streetwise than the kids at the local primary school I see opposite my house these days, clambering in and out of Chelsea tractors driven by stressed parents competing daily to grab the parking space nearest to the entrance. I recently remarked to the head teacher that they should adopt a drive-through arrangement, like McDonalds. Fortunately he thought it was funny.

The only really bad thing that happened to me in the junior school was that at the age of eight, my eyesight collapsed. The first mum knew about it was when she was called in to the school because I was disrupting classes. It turned out that this was because I could not read the blackboard, and my teacher suspected something was wrong with my eyesight. In fact I was just asking the kid next to me what the teacher was writing up there.

The upshot was that I was taken off to the NHS optician, a bus ride away. He diagnosed an infection, prescribed some evil-smelling ointment, and when the infection subsided, tested my eyesight regularly over a long period, then prescribed a series of spectacles which gradually allowed the muscles in my eyes to rebuild themselves. Thank you, sir, whoever you were. And thank you NHS, still in its infancy at the time.

All this took time of course, and I missed months of schooling. When I did go back, I was put into a class a year below my former classmates. I was far from happy, mainly because I had missed out on being with the best liked teacher in the school, Mr Valentine, who was really cool and played the guitar. Instead I was in Mrs Rooney's class, and I thought she was soppy. This spurred me on to make great efforts to catch up, which I did by halfway through the year, when I was upgraded and put back into my proper year group, with Mr Valentine. I lost a girlfriend too. She didn't like my glasses. I think her name was Pat.

But then I had other health problems. My teeth were apparently not conforming to the generally accepted norms of dental propriety, largely, I now suspect, because of the wicked Corona man, and the cavalier way in which some of my teeth were yanked out at the slightest provocation by the NHS dentist from hell. She was a short stout red-faced Sottish woman with a habit of repeatedly ordering 'Open Big', which even I knew was ungrammatical. Things went from bad to worse until the day when she said 'bite' before she had removed her finger from my ravaged mouth. So I obeyed. Honestly, it was not deliberate, but it did feel quite satisfying, like gristle. Now I was in real trouble.

By then my remaining teeth were sprouting out in all directions, apparently, so I was measured up for a 'plate', designed to bring them to order. The demon dentist said if I didn't have one now, I would be ugly and never get married. Once installed, it became the bane of my young life. I eventually got barred from the NHS clinic after throwing the tantrum to end all tantrums and refusing treatment, so I was registered with a suitably stern male private dentist. When I turned up with a damaged plate, he suggested I had broken it playing football. I was offended not by being accused of carelessness, but because of the football reference, a sport which he really ought to have known I hated. Poor research, obviously.

Sorry mum, I know you could hardly afford private treatment.

Despite these little setbacks I managed somehow to get into the top class in time for the eleven plus. This class was the exclusive domain of possibly the weirdest teacher ever to strut the stage of a primary school assembly hall, and probably one of the best intentioned, I gather. His pedagogy was built on the three sturdy pillars of swot, physical training (PT) and corporal punishment. Deluded, but according to my mum, a man who meant well.

I did my best! I really did, but however hard I tried, I was always in trouble. He just had it in for me. The idea that being assaulted by an adult with a cane could enhance learning or understanding in a child remains incomprehensible and repugnant to me, but I think this weirdo really believed in it. He caned me over twenty times that year, until my mum found the courage to blow the whistle on him after she noticed my bruises.

Now a confession. In my last year I became an active playground fighter. I was small but fast. Survival in the primary school depended on being a member of one of two gangs, at war with each other. I think we were brainwashed by war films and cowboy stories. No boy could opt out. I chose Bobby Bowman's gang because he promised to look after me.

The only fight I remember was, ironically, with a fellow Bobby's gang member, not the enemy. Seymour, he was called. He was small too, and he was in the habit of snatching my glasses off my nose and running off, taunting me to come and get them. He was fast too, but one day I caught him and bashed him in a blind fury, which he was not expecting. Nor did I, for that matter. When the others caught us up I had him squirming on the dusty tarmac, and he was losing the battle. You can't beat the element of surprise. Mr Valentine was on play-duty and tore us apart before much blood was spilt. I can't remember what happened to my glasses or whether we were punished. I do remember Mr Valentine asking me what on earth had got into me, requiring us to shake hands. After the fight Seymour and I became good pals. I suppose my status in the gang must have improved, because I became Bobby's number two for a while, specs and all. I don't think Mr Valentine told my mum and dad about my short-lived career as a playground scrapper, but mum must have suspected foul play from the state of me at home time. She has never mentioned it, and nor have I.

Anyway, I managed somehow to sneak through the ridiculous and divisive eleven plus exam. I gather marks were added for younger children at that time. And so in 1954 I was bound for grammar school, where I never fought or got the cane again.

Chapter 9 | Getting by

Transcript: Episode 5 of a series of podcasts recorded during the third Covid-19 lockdown, 2021. Written and read by Tom Dobson.

1947 - 1953

When we moved into our prefab, most families on the estate were down on their uppers. For some reason I thought the man we called Dad was a postman, but at some point, I must have discovered that he was a bus conductor. I remember the wonderful weekly event when he came home and put his wage packet on the kitchen table, a small brown packet with real pounds and coins inside. The figure of seven pounds a week is embedded in my brain. I think this was that was his wage in the mid-fifties. That's £241.43 today, £12,554.36 a year after taxes. To feed and house a family of four. Not much left over at the end of the week. Sometimes he worked overtime, earning a bit more. Mum and dad never went into debt, and we never went short of food. Somehow they must have saved enough for holidays, at first with relatives, later in a bed and breakfast at the seaside.

The war had its legacy too. Ingenuity was at a premium, and dad was nothing if not ingenious. At the back of the prefab, on the roadside, was an Anderson shelter. Every prefab had one. Originally designed as bomb shelters, these corrugated iron structures were now at the disposal of all estate tenants, officially to be used as coal bunkers. But dad decided he needed a workshop, so he went about building a lean-to coal shed next to the shelter, to free it up for storing tools and mending things. The idea was OK, but there were just two snags, no materials, and no money. Undaunted, he found a solution. We didn't know what he was really up to at the time, but it turned out he was making a Heath Robinson wheelbarrow out of a disused wooden box mounted on a scrap pram chassis. At least I hope it was disused. Charlie and I were the first beneficiaries, as dad pushed us around in the barrow at dangerous speeds, on test runs. Phase one of dad's cunning plan.

One day he said he was going to take us out for a trip further afield. I'm not sure where we went, but it must have been quite a way from the estate. After taking turns at pushing the barrow, we arrived at a building site where private houses were in various states of construction. Dad had evidently been monitoring progress on the quiet. I'm sure we didn't have to break in. What dad was after were broken bricks, lying discarded on the ground. They were destined to be our brave new coal shed. I think it took a few barrowloads, but soon we had enough to do the job. Phase two accomplished.

Apparently this kind of activity was not regarded as theft in those post-war days, more like waste management. Years later dad told me that this was an example of the elegant art of scrounging, not necessarily confined to ex-servicemen. He also said he had an arrangement with the builders anyway. OK dad.

As to where the sand and cement came from, dad claims to have forgotten long ago. Several other dads had the same idea, and brick coal sheds quietly appeared around the estate. From time to time they would come round under cover of darkness to borrow dad's barrow, now a legend in its own right. Sadly, a few years later, dad's ingenuity was to be his undoing.

As for the coal shed itself, it wasn't pretty, but it did the job. It was the bane of our life. Charlie and I were charged with going out back in all weathers to fill the coke hod and lug it into the front room to keep the stove going. (Coke as in distilled coal, not the stuff some people put their noses.)

Mum did her best to keep us going too. As far as I know, she had little or no prior experience of gardening, but we had one of the bigger gardens because we were on a corner plot, so she established a thriving vegetable and fruit garden out back. I have a vague recollection that she was helped by her elder brother Albert, who lived a few miles away. Her horticultural secret weapon was horse manure. This came for free, delivered almost to the door, courtesy of the milkman's horse. However, the competition was fierce, as neighbours had the same idea. Every day, anxious mums on the estate would be waiting behind their doors to pounce, shovels at the ready, praying that the horse would decide to drop his load outside their house. There would be the occasional altercation if two or more arrived at the steaming pile at the same time.

For some reason mum used to keep the rotting manure in the old zinc bath that came with us from the old house. She came up with the idea of adding pints of water to the dung, to produce liquid manure. It must have worked – her spuds, cabbage and runner beans were the envy of many. Not to mention the roses. If she could have, she would have kept a few hens too but that was prohibited.

Unfortunately, one day I became the accidental victim of the manure bath. It was a hot summer and we had one of our aunties and her family over, and my uncle had the great idea of chasing us and our cousins with the hose pipe. When I backed away from the water jet, the rim of the tin bath caught me behind my knees and I ended up arse first in the reeking liquid, unable to get out. Merriment all round. I tried my best to laugh it off, but what I remember most was that having been hosed down on the lawn, I had to wear a pair of girl's knickers for the rest of the day. The humiliation stays with me still. Mary claims to this day they were her knickers, borrowed from next door. I didn't know much about girls, but I knew enough to find this shameful. Mind you, we used to share a bath with Mary sometimes, so I'm not sure why I felt that way.

Another family, the Bignalls, whose garden backed on to the woods, did keep chickens. Mr Bignall, due to previous rationing, bought the chickens for the purpose of eating and he used to have a weird metal contraption that went round the chicken's neck to kill it humanely. However, it didn't always work as planned. I remember seeing chickens running around their garden with their necks and heads dangling over, dead but still mobile. Mrs Bignall then had the job of plucking the chicken. It used to be hung over the coal shed door so she could pull all the feathers out which would fly all over the place. She didn't like doing this, but it obviously needed to be done before the chicken could be roasted for Sunday dinner.

Charlie and I liked the Bignalls. Their Dad seemed to be around more than ours, and their mum was really nice to us. She was also beautiful. Occasionally we were allowed to play with their kids, Janet and Jamie, and even have our tea at their place. Mrs Bignall also had the temerity to be fashionable, and she went out to work, almost unheard of. The clincher was, they had a TV. I think they may have bought it specially for the event of the decade, the coronation, and we had been invited to watch it.

We have all seen those grainy black and white flickering TV images and heard Mr Dimbleby's hushed tones as he delivered his sober commentary, ad infinitum. For me, it's hard to disentangle what we were seeing from the actual experience of watching live TV, crammed into the Bignalls' front room, with someone manipulating the indoor aerial whenever anybody in the room dared to move. Mrs Bignall tried to keep our interest, plying us with pop and cakes, but it was uphill work. It was all so slow. This event had been billed as something exciting, but we were disappointed when it was simply boring. But after that we became guest TV watchers despite the usual warnings about square eyes, addicts for a while. Muffin the mule, Andy Pandy, Sooty, Bill and Ben. All that. It was a step up from children's programmes on the wireless, but we still used to listen to them over the years. Starting with Listen with Mother and ending with Counterpoint and Journey into Space.

To be honest, what we really looked forward to most was the weekly arrival on the estate of the Corona Lorry. Nothing to do with viruses. It was a vision of loveliness, an open sided truck, piled high with multicoloured bottles of pop, fizzy drinks specifically designed to rot children's teeth. Dad's theory was that Corona was owned by a consortium of evil dentists, masquerading as Thomas & Evans Ltd. We were strictly rationed of course. My favourites were Tizer, cherryade and Dandelion and Burdock. Charlie liked American Soda, but I hated it. I think all the kids collected the metal caps that kept the bubbles in. Collecting stuff was the thing then, and swapping was a serious matter. I think we made badges out of them too. The age of innocence and tooth decay.

Chapter 10 | Spare the child

1953

A grey November day. Nothing but rain for days. Now it's drumming on the corrugated roof and streaming down the windows. Olive is in the kitchen, washing up. She catches sight of Tom through the internal window, as he emerges from the bathroom into the front room, to stand in front of the fire, wrapped in a towel.

'Where on earth did you get those bruises? Has that Mr Denton been giving you the cane again?'

Tom is embarrassed. He's been trying hide the marks on his backside for days, but this time his towel has just slipped. 'It's nothing mum, don't tell dad. Please.'

Olive is furious. 'Let me see. This isn't right. Can't be much of a teacher that man. Don't you worry. Just get you're your pyjamas on. What about Charlie? Does he get the cane?

'I think he has, once or twice, but he's not in Mr Denton's class.'

'Does he know you've had the cane? Charlie, I mean.'

'Yes mum. But loads of boys get it too, it's not just me.'

'Do you think you deserve it? Do you misbehave? Are you cheeky or something?

'No mum, not really. It's mostly when I make mistakes.'

'What kind of mistakes? You mean mistakes in your work? Like getting your sums wrong or something like that?'

'Yes, mostly, but I can never tell when it's going to happen. I think he's just got it in for me.'

'Well, what was it for last time?'

'We all had these cardboard strips and we had to use them to make three columns in our arithmetic books and our English books. They're different sizes. There was one strip for the arithmetic book and another for the English book and I got them muddled up, so I rubbed them out and started again. The rubber made a mess, so he sent me out for the cane.'

Olive is even more furious. 'That's ridiculous. Everyone makes mistakes. I can't have this.'

'Once before, he gave me the cane for something Jack Mellor did. When he was lecturing me in the cloakroom I said he'd got the wrong boy, and he realised he'd made a mistake, so he got Jack out and caned him. Then he said well I'm going to cane you too, for the next time you do something wrong.'

Olive is almost in tears now. 'My God. Sorry Tom but I will have to talk to Dad about this. It's not right.'

Tom just sighs, fights back his tears, goes off to bed and pretends to read his Eagle comic. Charlie looks up from his Beano.

'Don't worry. She won't let Dad go mad this time. It's not your fault and I'll stick up for you. He's a bloody bastard that Denton.'

Harry is on late shift today, and when he comes home, Olive tells him what has happened. 'He's putting on a brave face, but I think this caning is getting him down. I don't want to make matters worse, but I agree, we've got to complain. What makes me mad is Tom's not a bad boy. He's just a bit careless at times. You know what his last teacher said about him – he's a dreamer. His mind is somewhere else half the time. Is it a crime, to be a dreamer? I think we should ask to see the headmaster, don't you?'

Tucking into his steak and kidney pudding, Harry struggles to get his head around all this. 'Did you know about all this caning before?'

'Yes, but I never dreamed it had got to this. Bruises on his backside – that's just cruelty. We don't hit our boys, so I don't think he should. Please don't go off the deep end with Tom like you used to do. He's still a bit afraid of you, so it would only make it worse.'

'I know. I'm sorry love. I promised you I wouldn't shout at him again, and I meant it. It's just I get so tired. But if I get near this Denton bugger I'll find it hard to keep my temper. I think we should ask to see the punishment record book first, that might kick them up the arse.'

This comes as news to Olive. 'Does that mean they have to record every punishment?'

'I think so. In theory anyway. I must have read about it in some novel, so I might have got it wrong. Could just be in those posh public schools. No harm in asking anyway, might be enough to stop him in his tracks. All right, I'll write to the headmaster now and ask to see the punishment book and demand a meeting.'

Olive posts the letter the next day. It's addressed to the headmaster, Mr Potter.

The headmaster writes back quite promptly, saying that he has consulted Mr Denton and the school denies any allegation that Tom has been maltreated. He also reminds Olive and Harry that corporal punishment is not unlawful in England, and that it is an accepted disciplinary measure, widely practised in the British education system as an effective method of correcting bad behaviour in boys. He makes no response to the request to see the punishment book. The meeting never happens.

Olive is outraged. 'So what do we do now?'

Harry has his head in his hands. He's pretty good at fighting his corner at work, but he hasn't seen this one coming. 'I suppose we could get a lawyer on the case, but I don't think we'd have a leg to stand on. Anyway we couldn't afford it. It goes against the grain to give in, but let's just see if Tom gets the cane again. My bet is he won't.

In any case he'll be going to secondary school soon, and we shouldn't do anything to put him off passing the eleven plus. It's all wrong, but there it is.'

Harry is right. Tom is never caned again, nor is Charlie. To everyone's surprise, including his own, Tom passes the eleven plus.

Olive is overwhelmed, to the point of embarrassing Tom with a hug. 'How about that then? Well done Tom. Just imagine, our son going to the Grammar School.'

Harry is typically reserved in his praise. 'Good for you Tom. That'll show a few of them round here.'

There's knock on the door. It's Agnes, Mary and Bill from next door, full of the good news. Harry and Olive bask in the limelight and the grownups celebrate with pale ale and Babycham. Corona pop for the kids. Charlie glows with pride for his brother, while Tom does his best to look modest. Mary tries to kiss Tom, but he manages to dodge the worst. Olive vows to bake her best chocolate cake for the weekend. Bill promises to organise an outing for them all, and they all troop off to Kew Gardens a week later. The novelty has worn off for Tom and he's given up the modest hero act. He's found out that a girl up the road is going to get a brand-new bike as a reward for passing the exam, so he asks for one too. Worth a try.

Harry is worried about the financial implications. The uniform and all that will cost a fortune, never mind a bike. He keeps his concerns to himself for the moment.

Many years later, when Tom is a teacher himself, he becomes active in a long running campaign against corporal punishment in schools and refuses to inflict any kind of corporal punishment on children himself. This alienates him in the staff room, and does his career no good at all, but he is adamant.

Corporal punishment in UK schools is not outlawed until 1986.

Chapter 11 | The hill

Transcript: Episode 6 of a series of podcasts recorded during the third Covid-19 lockdown, 2021. Written and read by Tom Dobson.

1950 - 1955

My brother Charlie reminded me recently that one of the accidental benefits of prefab life, for us at least, was the semi-rural setting, with trees, a pond and what seemed like open country, all within walking or running distance. Though we lived only a few miles from London we learned to climb trees, have adventures, light fires and fall through the ice on the pond, unsupervised. It made for a happy childhood while it lasted.

From our bedroom window we could see Abbey Hill through the woods that formed part of the estate boundary. Some of those who were lucky enough to live in the prefabs that backed straight on to the woods had unofficial back gates. Otherwise, it meant a long walk round to the stile on the main road. By the time I went up to the big school, Dad had given up on the going out ban, and during the long holidays, Abbey Hill was where it all happened. A place for boys to play at Robin Hood or Cowboys and Indians. No real horses, but bags of imagination. I'm not sure what the girls got up to.

Though the prefab estate is no more, Abbey Hill is now designated as a Country Park, and a new housing development has been built where some of the prefabs were sited, including ours. It's rather lovely – small redbrick apartment blocks, discreetly surrounded by trees.

I share the recollection of fishing for tiddlers in the pond, but my principal memory is of falling through the winter ice there. We used to have proper winters back then, and even grown-ups used to skate on the ice. Worse than the shock of freezing water was the experience of sloshing my way home, the long way round, shivering like a drowned rat. I can't remember the reception I got at home. Just as well.

An even more shameful memory from when I was about fifteen is of a disgraceful craze involving the possession of an air pistol. My mum and dad never knew I had one. I cannot remember buying it, but I do remember saving up the money, earned by washing posh people's cars at weekends. Some boys bragged that they used their air guns to shoot birds or rabbits, but I was horrified by that, so there used to be a tournament at the pond, aiming at sinking a disused tin can. How we never got caught I'll never know.

During my first year at the big school I became friends with a second-year boy, possibly the most disruptive in the school. He lived a few miles away but once or twice he came over for the day, travelling by train. We used to hang out on the hill, climbing trees, making up stories and so on. My mum would make up a packed lunch. Few will remember Ivor – he was a stranger to other kids on the estate. He used to come over from his house mainly to escape from his strict Scottish mother and her brood of irritating kids. One of our favourite games was pretending to be American. We used to pretend we were the sons of a Yankee airman working at a nearby air base, putting on American accents. Not very credible, especially as Ivor had bright red hair and freckles and our imitated accents were rubbish.

We were great fans of the Goon Show and we took great delight in imitating Eccles, Bloodnock, Bluebottle and co, much to the irritation of any adults within earshot. Strange to hear the goons back again on four extra. I used to get to school by train, and Ivor lived further out of London on the same line. We used to entertain bored passengers with our version of the goons, making rude noises, talking American and generally behaving badly. Nobody ever shut us up, but we had our share of glares.

At school, Ivor introduced me to the delights of playing the harmonica, and with another boy, George, we formed a short-lived harmonica band. We used to entertain commuters with that too. My train ride was only one station away, but Ivor and George were farther away. Ivor used to bring his instrument when he came over to the prefab, and we used to rehearse and jam up on the hill too. The only tune I remember is Three Bells:

'There's a village in the valley
Among the pine trees half forlorn
And there on a sunny morning
Little Jimmy Brown was born (bong bong bong bong)

All the chapel bells were ringing
In the little valley town
And the song that they were singing
Was for baby Jimmy Brown

Then the little congregation
Prayed for guidance from above
'Lead us not into temptation
Bless this hour of meditation
Guide him with eternal love'

Ivor's family were religious. We got pretty good at this number.

Prefabulous Days

One day Ivor said he'd heard there was some kind of secret spy observation post somewhere on the hill. By now I knew every tree, puddle and bush up there, but this was a new one on me. I checked around and it turned out he was half right. There was such a thing, and various boys had claimed to have broken in. It wasn't on the hill itself, but on nearby farmland. In fact on a fine day you could see the small compound and a hut from our hill. We hatched our own plan to get in. The farm was on private land of course, but we had no difficulty finding the hut. Of course we couldn't get into the fenced compound, so we gave it up as a bad job.

No matter. We made up an elaborate story which goes something like this: Having made sure nobody was about, we broke in using a key which we'd found in the nearby woods. As we went in, we saw a hatch, which we lifted with ease, and underneath, a ladder that led down into the bunker. As we climbed down, lights came on automatically, and we could hear a faint hum, which got louder as we descended. At the bottom we found ourselves in a kind of control room, equipped with all kinds of consoles with flickering screens, and telephones. There were bunks too and some locked cabinets. A loudspeaker hissed. It smelled of tobacco and sweat.

I think we must have got all this nonsense from the Eagle comic. Nobody believed us of course, but in fact, as it turns out, we were not too far off the mark. The hut had been part of a network of military observation posts during the Second World War, operated by the Royal Observation Corps to spot approaching formations of German bombers, tracking their movements once they were over Britain. The ROC men reported directly to Fighter Command HQ on the type and number of planes they could see, and the direction they were flying.

It turns out that a few years later, the station was upgraded to monitor faster jet aircraft, and in the sixties, a bunker was indeed built underground. It apparently consisted of two rooms, a monitoring room and a storeroom (with a chemical toilet in it). The Cold War was then at its height, and in an emergency the job of these observation posts would be to report where nuclear bombs had exploded, and to monitor the spread and toxicity of the radioactive fallout. Two or three observers would be expected to seal themselves into the bunker, and stay there, potentially for many weeks. So there - our stupid adolescent fantasy wasn't so daft after all.

Our made-up story had an odd spin-off. We decided to set up our own observation post, in the woods behind the estate, not to monitor aircraft, but to spy on goings-on among its inhabitants. Instead of a hut, we had a tent, hidden in the woods, with a good view of the estate. One of my uncles donated a pair of ex-army binoculars, and we took it in turn to observe and make notes in a little black notebook. It didn't last long. Mainly because nothing happened. Well, nothing we could see anyway. We did sneak around the estate a bit and a few net curtains twitched, but still no juicy detective-type leads. We didn't even get told off, which was disappointing. Shame really, as in fact there was quite a bit of hanky-panky going on, by all accounts.

Ivor left the scene when he and his eccentric family emigrated to Australia. We corresponded by airmail for a while, but that fizzled out after a few years. I caught up with him quite recently, thanks to the miracle of the internet. He did remember our Abbey Hill larks, but never admitted the bunker episode, nor our own spy hideout. He had a clear recollection of the prefab and how nice my mum was.

After Ivor's vanishing act I acquired a girlfriend. Yes, a real girl, as distinct from the imaginary kind. She didn't live on the estate. Her name was Pat, and we had known each other from primary school days. By this time I did know about sex, but my mum had made it clear that sex before marriage was strictly out of question. To be honest, I was simply scared anyway. Her dad had an ironmongery in town, and the family had a holiday home on an island called Hamhaugh Island, on the Thames. I spent a weekend there once, wishing I could swim. Her Dad didn't like me much, but her mum was very nice to me, and I liked her. She made great pies for tea. In the good weather, Pat and I used to go on quite long walks on the hill and in the woods. We would sometimes stop at the pond to eat picnic lunches made up by our unknowing mums. Or we thought they were unknowing. I found out much later that they both knew what was going on, and, to their credit, kept it to themselves. My dad hadn't a clue, and Charlie and I had sworn a lifetime oath never to grass on each other.

This chaste affair only lasted two summers, mainly due to her best friend Nora, who made a point of playing gooseberry whenever possible. I think she was jealous. She called me a squirt. Pat failed the eleven plus and so went to the local secondary modern.

We simply drifted apart. I sometimes wonder what became of Pat, my first love, up there on the hill.

Chapter 12 | A spot of bother

1955 / 1958

The trouble starts when Olive assumes that their cat Suki has been attacked by Mrs Payne's bull terrier Mathilda. The Paynes' prefab is situated right opposite the Dobsons' on the other side of Friars Walk. Their front door faces the Dobsons' side door, as the street curves right, with the Green Thing rising from the pavement between the two prefabs.

It's true that the Paynes haven't a clue about dog training, and Mathilda has proved a determined and skilled canine escape artist. To be fair, they have tried, tethering her outside or keeping her indoors. The usual cause of her escapades is their younger son George's habit of leaving doors and gates open. To his mother Angharad, neither he nor Mathilda can do any wrong. It's true that Suki does come home one day, wounded, and Mathilda creeps home with some impressive scratches to her muzzle. Circumstantial evidence.

At any rate, Suki sleeps it off, as cats do, but Olive is a bit upset. When Harry comes home after work and the boys have gone to bed, she mentions the Mathilda versus Suki episode.

Harry doesn't want to stir up trouble. 'Well, these things happen love. If it happens again, I'll have a word with Dennis. The dog's just a puppy, and she doesn't bite as far as I know. She just wants to get out and play with the kids. Sounds like she's learned about cats the hard way.'

'Dennis? Oh, you know him then?'

'Well, not really. We do bump into one another occasionally. He works for his father at Paynes Hardware in Watford. He had a rough time in the Indian Army apparently.'

'And I suppose you know her name too?'

'He calls her Angharad. It's Welsh.'

'I see. Now I know. She's a bit stand-offish with me. Not too sure about the boy, but I like Pete. He's such a nice young bloke.'

'Live and let live, I say' Says Harry.

Talk of the devil, some weeks later, Pete, the older Payne son, turns up at the Dobsons', as he usually does when he's home on leave. Harry's at work, but the boys are home from school. They like Pete. He tells them stories about soldiering and regularly produces goodies from faraway places. German beers for Harry, make up or perfume for Olive, weird toys and chocolate bars for the boys. Soon he's enjoying a well mashed mug of good old British tea, milk and three sugars. Charlie clamours for some more thrilling stories, and Pete's glad to comply, hopefully without revealing too many military secrets, while Olive listens from the kitchen.

Just as Pete is getting in his stride, they are interrupted by the sound of Mathilda, barking outside.

'Oh heck, she must have escaped again. Trying to find me I guess. Hang on, I'll get her.'

Pete and the boys run outside. They can hear Mathilda, but at first they can't see her. Charlie's the first to spot the excited dog. 'She's on the roof, look. She must have run up Dad's ladder'.

Sure enough, Mathilda is scrambling and slithering about on the corrugated roof, wailing like a banshee. When she sees Pete, she slides down to the top of the ladder Harry has left at the back of the prefab, still propped up where he's been clearing the gutter.

Charlie is delighted, but Tom is worried. Olive just shrugs and closes the kitchen door behind them. By this time, the kids from the Green Thing gang have gathered on the pavement, cheering and jeering. 'Hey Mathilda! You learning to ski or something?'

Pete's in stitches but feels it's his job to get this barmy dog down, so he starts to climb the ladder, but Mathilda just runs back up to the top of the roof, still wailing. After several attempts to entice Mathilda down, Pete gives up.

'She'll get down on her own if we leave her be. Come on, let's get back indoors.'

Even Olive is laughing when they come in. 'Daft dog, that, Pete. I didn't know dogs could climb ladders. Harry's fault really, leaving it there like that.'

For a while, they can hear Mathilda scampering about on the roof, then it goes quiet. Led by Pete, they all creep out, to see her whimpering at the top of the ladder. Climbing up was easy enough, but she seems afraid to come down. Pete put his finger to his lips, then climbs slowly up, gets hold of her and brings her gently down. When peace is restored and Mathilda is sitting in the Dobson's front room as if nothing has happened, Pete apologises and makes a move. At the kitchen door, he turns to Olive. 'I almost forgot. I've got some news for you. I don't think I'll be back again for a while. I've met a lovely girl. We plan to emigrate. Canada probably.'

Olive smiles. 'Congratulations! Sounds like a plan Pete. Hope it works out for you. New life – wonderful. I sometimes wish we'd emigrated. Hope to meet your wife one day.'

Pete smiles, salutes the boys, gives a thumbs-up, shakes Olive by the hand.

The only one around who has not been affected by all this rumpus is Suki, who slumbers happily on Charlie's bed.

Olive puts Harry in the picture that night.

'I always seem to miss the fun round here. Sounds like a laugh. Hope it hasn't damaged the roof.'

'Well, your fault for leaving that ladder there. At least she didn't poo up there like she does in my borders.'

They don't see Pete again until 1958, when Arthur Payne, Dennis's father, dies of a heart attack. Mathilda dies in sympathy. Soon after, the Paynes simply disappear. Their prefab is empty. The word is they now live in a council house in Rickmansworth. Arthur has left the business to Pete, who returns from Canada, complete with lovely wife, posh car and twin girls.

Harry grins at this news. 'Smart lad, that Pete.'

Olive has been thinking it all over. 'You know what, looking back, I wouldn't be surprised if that Angharad was so stand-offish because of that manure business, you know, when I used to beat her to the horse muck. It was a bit of a joke at the time, when we all used to rush out behind Jim the milkman's horse to shovel up all that lovely poo, fresh and steaming. But she used to get miffed when she didn't get in first. It got so silly in the end that me and the other girls stayed back and let her have it her own way. I reckon she's borne a grudge ever since.'

A rather pleasant Irish family called Byrne moves in over the road. They have identical twin girls who quickly charm the entire neighbourhood. Niamh hits it off with Olive and Agnes. Bill secretly fancies Niamh. Olive secretly fancies

Patrick. Agnes too, maybe. Drink is taken and a new year is welcomed in. Harry develops a liking for Guinness. The local kids still hang out at the Green Thing, but now they show disturbing signs of adolescence. Peace descends once more on this corner of the estate.

Chapter 13 | Holidays

Transcript: Episode 7 of a series of podcasts recorded during the third Covid-19 lockdown, 2021. Written and read by Tom Dobson.

1950 - 1970

Until the mid-fifties saving up for a summer holiday was out of the question, on my dad's meagre wages. No credit cards or overdrafts in those days. If you didn't have the cash, you went without. We didn't have money, but we did have relatives. The first holiday I remember was split between two relatives, both living in Norfolk. The first week was in Acle, mum's family village, staying with one of her sisters, Alice, and the second week was with my dad's eldest brother James and his wife Brenda, in Great Yarmouth.

My memories of both weeks are hazy. Alice worked in the village shop, and her husband John was a farm labourer. We stayed in their small terraced house. They had no children, so Mum and dad slept in their spare bedroom while Charlie and I had camp beds downstairs in the front room. I recall tractor rides, mucking out pigs, free sweets at the shop, numerous walks in the countryside and a shopping trip to Norwich, where we had a picnic by a river and went to a castle. We had no car, so we got the bus, and dad had a good chat with the conductor. Comparing notes.

As usual, Charlie fell asleep there and back. Mum bought a souvenir mug each for us. Charlie chose the one with a picture of the castle, and I got the one with the cathedral. I don't think mum bought anything for herself, it was all window shopping really. I suppose it must have been the first time Charlie and I ever walked provincial city streets. We couldn't have picked a finer city.

That's it really. Being in the countryside was not that much of a novelty for us as our prefab estate was close to green fields and woods anyway. Alice did try to pair us up with a couple of girls who lived down the road, and we had a picnic with them, but the only thing I remember is that they were sun-tanned and giggled a lot. They were twins, I think. They had a pram each, with dolls in them, just like the girls we knew at home. They wore gumboots and flowery frocks and they seemed keen on doing cartwheels, showing off their matching knickers. That kind of image stays in the mind.

The second week was something of a disaster, mainly because Charlie and I got bored, and Brenda was horrible to us. Uncle James was a great old bloke, and he made an effort to entertain us with stories about his time in the Boer war and ice creams on the prom, but Brenda seemed to resent us all being in their house. They had decorated our bedroom, and we got into trouble right from the start by making a mess on the wallpaper. Her cooking was awful, so we had a lot of fish and chips in town, with James, who seemed to prefer being out of the house. He used to laugh about Brenda, gently mocking her Norfolk accent. She called soap soup and talked about going to the poost awfice to buy stamps. Brenda chain smoked, reeked of perfume, dyed her hair blonde, and swore a lot. Of an evening she would disappear to the pub and return drunk. Mum explained to me later that Brenda was much younger than James, and was, in her opinion, a godless tart who was living off poor James' war pension, topped up with immoral earnings. Never one to beat about the bush, our mum. Years later poor old James died of syphilis, or so mum reckoned. No idea what happened to Brenda.

On the plus side, we built a lot of sandcastles, discovered seaside rock with letters through it and watched women mending fishing nets at Lowestoft. James would join in. We probably returned with sun tans.

As time went on, it became very clear that dad didn't much like holidays. He rarely exposed his skin to the sun and only paddled in the sea with rolled-up trousers under protest. At the beach he preferred to hire a deckchair and read his News Chronicle. He hated ice-cream because it gave him toothache, and he was wary about eating out, especially after I knocked over a cup of tea in a crowded café. However these idiosyncrasies were as nothing to his fear of trains. Siderodromophobia it's called apparently. He was absolutely certain we would crash or be derailed.

The business of getting to and returning from holiday destinations were at once farcical and unbearable for Olive. It started with the meticulous packing of brown cardboard cases. Each had to be locked, bound with stout rope, double tied and sealed with red sealing wax. His other obsession was the absolute certainty that the tickets would be lost or fall down the gap between the train and the platform. When the great day came and we would lug all our stuff on buses, tube trains and mainline steam trains, Charlie and I would be in stitches trying not to laugh out loud, while poor Olive cringed with embarrassment. Even when we managed to find a compartment, lifting the luggage on to the racks was yet more palaver.

Then, when under way, the little sliding windows had to be shut to avoid cinders from the engine blowing in, or the tickets being sucked out before Mum would break out the packed lunches. Her speciality was egg and tomato sandwiches which, once unwrapped, would stink in the confined space of the stuffy closed compartment. Something to do with the acid in the tomatoes reacting with the egg yolk, apparently. The most effective way of repelling fellow travellers ever devised. Give mum her due, she never gave in on this habit, despite our groans, farting noises and nose-pinching gestures. The strange thing was that though they smelled so bad, they tasted great when you were starving.

Then, when we neared our destination, Dad's luggage and ticket ritual would start up again, endangering the lives, limbs and sanity of all concerned, including fellow passengers.

Much later, when my parents managed to save up for a holiday that didn't involve relatives, we went to the Isle of Wight, to stay in a guest house in Shanklin. Getting there was even worse than usual because the journey included the ferry ride. Perhaps the tickets would somehow fall into the Solent, or maybe Charlie or I would be swept overboard. Or the ship would sink. Travel abroad upped the risk of disaster by several notches.

Once safely installed, we discovered we shared a surname with the landlady, Miss Charlotte Dobson. Not only that, but dad also proudly introduced her as a grand-niece of Old Dobbo, Dad's grandfather, the almost famous London music-hall performer. Dad had kept it secret, even from mum, as a surprise. The guest house was not exactly four-star, but dad had got a good deal as a long-lost relative. Charlotte had never married, so for a week we were the family she never had. We were blatantly favoured over other guests, with rooms overlooking the ocean and deluxe breakfasts, free afternoon teas in a café run by one of her pals in the high street and even a discounted meal for four in a fish restaurant on the prom. For once the holiday was worth the torture of getting there, and dad was a hero for a week. His only mistake was grabbing a cactus in some botanic gardens. My discoveries were mushrooms and yoghurt, dodgy foreign foods according to mum.

Another great holiday was in Hemsby, in Norfolk, staying in the caravan previously home to yet another relative. Caravan sites were pretty basic then, with only cold-water toilet facilities and no on-site entertainment. On this one there was a public address Tannoy which blared out the top ten between announcements. The number one that week was 'Diana', by Paul Anka:

I'm so young and you're so old
This, my darling, I've been told
I don't care just what they say
'Cause forever I will pray
You and I will be as free
As the birds up in the trees
Oh, please stay by me, Diana

Classic. The song quickly became an earworm which we missed when we went home. For the duration of the holiday it blew a typical Easterly gale, the scourge of the east coast, but we had a lot of fun nevertheless, as all kids do at the seaside. Dad didn't come with us this time. He would have hated it.

Aside from annual holidays, we didn't go short of day trips, mainly because dad had a free bus pass for all the family, valid with most bus companies. We were regular visitors to London attractions such as the Zoo in Regents Park and the museums in South Kensington. Charlie and I couldn't get enough of these outings, and mostly dad behaved himself. As usual mum supplied the packed lunches but by agreement the egg and tomato fillings had been replaced by cheese and pickle or sardines and tomato. Yum yum. The beauty of these trips was that they were unplanned, so if the sun shone, we could hop on a local bus and change on to the Greenline bus and take it from there. We were bus nomads, picnicking in the famous London parks, Regents, Hyde or St. James. Even snacking in Joe Lyons corner shop when resources allowed.

As things got slowly better money-wise, we ventured farther abroad. Because bus travel is relatively slow, this meant travelling by tube and train, but the main attraction was, as ever, the seaside. By careful timetable study, dad discovered we could be in Brighton by mid-morning, and back home by ten o'clock to collapse into bed at the prefab. Brighton Rock, a paddle, picnic on the beach or fish and chips, walk on the pier and make a dash for the train back to Victoria.

Happy days.

One time, Charlie was invited to go on holiday with Bill, Agnes and Mary next door. Bill had totally different connections, so their holiday destinations were equally different. By this time they had a Hillman Minx, so there was always a free ride in the offing. Charlie and Mary were the same age and always close friends. I had been offered a place, but I suppose I felt awkward, and in any case it would have been unbearable, five bodies in a Hillman Minx all the way to Dorset. They stayed in a holiday cottage near Bridport, owned by someone rich man who owed Bill a favour or two. Best not to ask. Neither Charlie nor Mary ever gave me a detailed account of this treat, but they returned even more suntanned and devoted to each other than they were before leaving the estate early one Saturday morning. I admit, I was envious of my brother, and of the bond between him and Mary. I was sure they would get married one day, but I was wrong.

Looking back, I realise that though we loved prefab life, we were relatively constrained. Holidays and day trips made all the difference, at least until Charlie and I got older. For me, there was a strange sequel. When I came home during the summer vacation at University, Mum and dad were about to go back to the Isle of Wight, a quiet caravan holiday. Charlotte had died, so they had booked in at a quite posh caravan site. The caravan slept four, and rather than stay on my own in the prefab, I asked if I could go along for the ride. It was one of the best holidays I've ever had. Me, a twenty-year-old undergraduate, with his mum and dad, talking about the past, walking, eating out, watching telly and drinking Guinness in the evenings. Funny, how your parents can become your friends when you've grown up a bit.

Chapter 14 | Partition

1947 - 1958

Like most brothers, Tom and Charlie fight. As soon as Charlie can toddle, he challenges Tom over possessions and attention. Olive is the arbiter most of the time, sometimes driven to lose her patience. Then Harry has to listen to her exasperation and is called in to mediate. They sometimes fall out over decisions and accuse each other of being too hard or too soft. All perfectly normal, especially in these days when dads are the breadwinners and mums are in charge at home when dads are away, breadwinning.

As the boys grow older, the main area of dispute is domestic territory. The prefabs are all two bedroomed, so the boys have to share one of them. As soon as Charlie is old enough to climb out of his cot, he covets Tom's bed, so a bunk bed is acquired. Of course, there is then a dispute over who will sleep on the top bunk. Tom wins that one, and Charlie sulks. The remaining floor space still must be shared. Tom is always willing to share almost everything with his baby brother, but not so Charlie. Much of the strife happens on rainy days when neither of them can play outside. Charlie almost always wins. He's physically the stronger and pulls no punches, literally. Tom usually concedes defeat first.

Once they are both at school, the situation changes. It becomes an uneasy truce, punctuated by occasional violations. As time goes on, Charlie prefers to spend more and more time outside, with the gang of neighbouring kids who congregate around the Green Thing. Tom is accepted as a kind of associate gang member, but he's quite happy to spend hours with his Meccano or reading a book. Harry buys them a second-hand desk each when Tom starts having homework, but neither of them lasts long. Tom does his work at the kitchen table and Charlie just pretends to do his. When Tom goes to grammar school, he flits between a variety of indoor hobbies, including model aeroplanes and boats, and examining all sorts of dead things with a small microscope his Uncle Albert has bought him. When confined, Charlie loves nothing better than helping Olive in the kitchen, drawing, painting and reading comics, or he goes next door to hang out with Mary. In the good weather he looks after his own garden or has adventures with the Green Thing gang in the woods or on the hill, with or without Mary.

Uncle Albert has always taken an interest in his sister Olive's children. Like her, he had migrated to London in search of work. His wife died young, and he was left with two sons. Albert notices Tom's interest in practical hobbies, and in particular his fascination with a Hobbies fretwork machine he bought his younger son, Basil. Tom asks his dad if he can have one, but they can't afford such things, and in any case, where would they put it? For Basil it has been a nine-day wonder, and he's happy to part with it, so one day it's installed it the boys' bedroom, in theory to be shared. Charlie is not in the least interested, so it becomes Tom's by default. It also becomes his obsession, and a problem.

If you've never seen one of these contraptions, imagine something a bit like a cross between a treadle sewing machine and a spinning wheel. It's a tripod with a treadle, hinged at the front, which drives a large, spiked drive wheel, which in turn powers an oscillating saw designed to take very fine blades, via a leather belt, a flywheel, and a connecting rod. The modern equivalent is an electric scroll saw. It was used to cut out patterns in pieces of thin wood, to make all kinds of decorative craft items from jigsaw puzzles to pipe racks and scale models.

It's hardly suited to a prefab bedroom. It's noisy and generates fine sawdust. A lot of it. The plywood Tom uses has quite a nice smell, but it gets everywhere. The fine dust takes a while to fall even in a still atmosphere. If there's the slightest draught, it turns up all over the house.

Then there's the difficulty of sourcing plywood with no budget, the costs of Hobbies Weekly magazine, and sawblades. Nevertheless Tom becomes adept at supplying all and sundry with decorous things, and the prefab has become a one-boy factory.

Among his best work is a model electric milk float, probably because on the prefab estate the former horse-drawn milk float has been replaced by one of these contraptions. He's painted it green and blue. His finest achievement is a complicated model of Princess Elizabeth's coronation carriage, but it's fragile and doesn't last long.

Then he discovers an ingenious way to produce marquetry, pictures made from different shapes cut out of wood veneers. The traditional way to cut the shapes is with a marquetry knife, but Hobbies have come up with an alternative method. Instead of cutting each element of the image with a sharp knife, he glues together a kind of sandwich of veneer sheets, each layer separated by a sheet of paper, then uses the fretwork machine to cut round each borderline just like making a jigsaw puzzle. He then soaks all the pieces to separate the layers, and carefully dries them. In this way, he can assemble as many final images as there are layers.

Despite being irritated by the sawdust everywhere, Olive is fascinated, and glad that Tom has become so adept and focused. Harry is worried by Tom's behaviour. 'Do you think it's good for him, sawing away in the bedroom all day long? I don't understand where he gets it from.'

'Well not from you, that's for sure. More likely it's from my side – he's taking after Albert. You must admit he's good at it, and it keeps him busy. He's saved us a bob or two on Christmas and birthday presents. So long as he's happy, I can't see any harm. The two of them are just different, that's all. Charlie's the outdoor type and Tom likes making things.'

This is not strictly true. Charlie makes things. Like pies, puddings and even a Sunday roast.

Harry perseveres with his argument. 'Well, it's such a mess in there, with all that sawdust and stuff. Not to mention that smelly glue and all the other things. Not much fun for Charlie, if you ask me.'

As he rides his bus one day, Harry comes up with an idea, a possible solution to the bedroom-cum-workshop problem. Why not sub-divide the boys' bedroom with a partition?

In typical Harry fashion, he starts work, measuring up, making drawings, buying or cadging timber. Olive has her doubts, but she keeps them to herself.

The construction of the prefab doesn't lend itself to this project. Fixing a new wall to the existing ones will be tricky, and one of the boys will always have to put up with the other going to and fro though his room. Despite the drawbacks, and given Harry's lack of experience, the result is more effective in containing the sawdust and giving the boys some privacy, than expected. Olive has long since abandoned any attempt to curb Harry's enthusiasms, and even Bill next door is impressed, which is very unusual. Charlie grumbles about not having the more private area. He concludes that the brother he had so admired when they were younger, has gone barmy, and there is little he can do except grumble.

But Harry's ingenuity is soon to be his downfall. The word about his partition gets around the estate. It seems the perfect solution to a different problem. By this time, neighbours with children of different sexes are worried about having teenage girls and boys sleeping in the same room. Some have applied for rehousing based on this understandable concern, but Harry's partition seems like a better idea. So from time to time a mum or dad drops round to see how he's done it. A few more partitions spring up around the estate. For a while, Harry is a local hero, glowing with justifiable pride in his new consultative role.

Then an inspector calls.

He's from the council. He says they have had a complaint about an alleged unauthorised structural alteration to the prefab. Under the terms of their tenancy agreement, he is required to carry out an internal inspection. It takes only a few minutes, and when Olive asks him whether there's a problem, he just says they will get a letter.

Sure enough, a buff envelope drops on the doormat a few days later. It contains an official notice instructing Harry to demolish and remove the partition within seven days, under pain of losing their right to live in the prefab.

Harry protests. 'How was I to know? And why would anyone complain? It doesn't harm the fabric of the building and it's nobody's business but ours.'

Olive looks out of the living room window. Such a lovely day. The sun shines bright on the neighbouring prefabs and their flourishing gardens. She sighs.

'If the Paynes hadn't done a flit, I don't think you'd need to look far for the complainer. Just open the side door'

'Of course! That Angharad. There's still her mate up the road. I'll.......'

'On no you won't. Just get that partition down. And let's apply for that transfer again, as soon as possible. We might get somewhere with a proper workshop.'

Not for the first time, the boys have worked out what has happened, so when Harry attempts to break the news, Tom has had a chance to agree with Charlie that they don't mind if the partition must go, they don't want to move to a new house.

'It's all right dad, I'll give up the fretwork if I have to. It's not fair on Charlie anyway.'

'But that's not fair on you, is it? I've been thinking. Maybe there's another way. How about we clear out the shelter and make it into a proper workshop. You could work out there. I only use it once in a blue moon. Maybe Bill could rig up a light or something for you.'

Bill says the best plan is just to run an extension lead out there from the kitchen when need be, with a transformer and circuit breaker. Any permanent wiring would need permission from the council, and you won't get that. 'You're on their radar now mate. Leave it to me.'

Bill and Harry remove the partition and use some of the timber to make shelving for Tom out in the shelter. In due course Uncle Albert replaces the old treadle mechanism with an electric motor kit for the fretwork machine, as a present. Tom prefers the treadle but goes on to use the machine to cut out parts for two guitars he makes for Charlie when he joins a skiffle group.

Sometimes Harry fantasises about getting his revenge on whoever grassed him up with the council. A least it helps him get off to sleep of a night.

Chapter 15 | Big School

Transcript: Episode 8 of a series of podcasts recorded during the third Covid-19 lockdown, 2021. Written and read by Tom Dobson.

1954 - 1961

My Mum and Dad were pleased that I had passed my eleven-plus, especially as I had missed best part of a year's schooling at Friarscroft Juniors when I nearly lost my eyesight. I learned later that for Dad, Grammar School entrance was a pretty big deal as he had always resented having been denied the opportunity himself, in favour of one of his brothers.

I also learned about the impact it had on my Dad's meagre wage packet. It meant finding money to kit me out with an expensive uniform, only obtainable from a posh tailor's shop which enjoyed a monopoly supplier arrangement with Canonsbury Grammar, the secondary school I was bound for. Regulation dress was compulsory – short trousers (grey), cap, tie, blazer, socks, badge. I never knew what the bill came to, but it was clear that the outlay came as a bombshell to my parents, already struggling to support themselves and two kids in a council prefab on a bus conductor's wage, probably around £12 per week in 1954 (about £312 today, 16,220 a year).

The uniform itself was typical of most English state Grammar school uniforms, memorable in this case only for its hideous colour scheme, brown and yellow. We looked like bees. Mums were expected to sew on the pocket badge which bore a pretentious Latin motto usually translated as 'Let us be judged by our deeds.' This may have been unfortunate, as in the early fifties at least, the school's reputation was marred by criminal behaviour of various types. If the deeds of the pupils were indeed to be judged, then the verdicts must have been a disappointment.

Schoolyard violence was evident from the start; fighting was the norm among the boys, and some of the girls were not averse to a scrap. As a small boy at primary school, I had a few playground skirmishes, and enjoyed them, but this aggression was in a quite different league. Teddy Boys were in fashion and knife-carrying was a mark of status. In one infamous gang-fight between the grammar school and the secondary modern over the way, serious injuries were inflicted, and the population of the nearest Borstal was duly augmented.

Apart from knives, the weapon of choice was the bicycle chain. I wonder to this day how neither school took preventative action. By lunchtime on the day most kids in both schools knew the fight was imminent and where the field of battle was to be. Some of us managed to keep out of harm's way by taking an alternative route home after school. This was tricky for me, as my brother Charlie went to Millers Way secondary modern. We talked about it beforehand, and he kept clear too. Of course the whole thing was hushed up.

Such problems were not uncommon, and rightly or wrongly, they have sometimes been attributed to the post-war effects of wartime evacuation and of rehousing schemes. Charlie and I knew several former evacuees whose families were re-housed on our prefab estate, but I have no evidence they were involved in criminal activities. One or two went to Canonsbury. Fortunately, these older boys left me alone, at school and on the estate. Perhaps there was some kind of prefab estate tribal loyalty in operation.

I learned later that school leadership was poor. Much was made at the time of the newly appointed headmaster who was hailed as a new broom, not only because he had a science qualification (Bachelor of Science!) but because he was relatively young. In fact he turned out to be a cane-wielding ex-army disciplinarian who commanded little respect among his younger staff. With hindsight I suspect he was simply out of his depth. Years later I came across him in Foyles bookshop, being pushed around in a wheelchair. He didn't remember me. Why would he?

For the first five years, the bane of my life was PT and games. They were compulsory. Mens sana in corpore sano. It wasn't so much the physicality I disliked, rather the encouragement of aggression and competition. The first PT master, Mr Titmus (ex-army), was allegedly dismissed for brutality, found guilty of routinely beating boys with a cricket bat. He was replaced by an equally unpleasant Rugby player, Mr Probert. I owe both of these men a great debt; they taught me (and a few others) how to outwit or avoid idiots in positions of authority.

It wasn't all bad of course. In the lower school I enjoyed English, French, German, art and music lessons. From time to time we were entertained by various quite imaginative japes initiated by senior pupils, such as replacing the school flag with a pair of industrial-grade women's knickers, jacking up the Geography master's car on bricks and removing the wheels, and, best of all, taking the new cricket scoring hut to bits and rebuilding it in the school hall.

I became interested in microbes for a while. I read library books about them and my parents gave me a junior microscope for my birthday, but it wasn't much good. Above all I loved woodwork and metalwork. Unfortunately, when the dreaded day arrived when we were all required to choose one out of several courses designed for success in the O-level examinations at the end of the fifth form, the rigidity of the curriculum could not cope with my eclectic mix of adolescent interests.

The Headmaster, being a science graduate, persuaded my parents that a maths and science course was my best bet, even though quite clearly I was no good at that kind of thing and there were no indications that I would ever be. The buzz word was technology. According to him it was wiser in the brave new post-war world to be a mediocre technologist than a good anything else. My own preferences were apparently irrelevant, and so I found myself condemned to two years being bamboozled by subjects like Physics, Maths, Applied Maths (whatever they were...) and Chemistry, all of which I either failed or dropped at O level. My only passes were in English Language, English Literature, French, and amazingly, Maths.

The Maths pass was a complete surprise. It was down mainly to an eccentric old-school type, Mr Bryce, who came up with the idea of filtering out mathematical dunces for remedial classes. His approach was to accept the fact that we were unable to comprehend mathematical concepts, and to second guess the exam questions. He just got us to learn by rote, each pupil having a personal tactical plan, designed around his or her least worst marks in classroom and homework tests. The headmaster also took over the classes when Mr Bryce was off sick. He turned out to be quite brilliant at explaining abstract concepts. I scraped though with the pass mark, 47%.

My best big school memory is the trip to France, the first time I ever went abroad. I had saved up for this trip from my earnings as a Saturday boy in Woolworths and Boots the Chemist. I think it cost around £25.

Standing on the deck of a Newhaven to Dieppe British Railways ferry, my first visual impression of France was a gendarme standing on the quayside at Dieppe, sporting a machine gun. Was it loaded? The second mental snapshot was of a group of French peasant women washing clothes in a river, seen from the SNCF steam train to Paris.

The official excuse for the school trip was that we could practice our conversational French. Needless to say, that didn't happen much, but for me it was the start of a love affair with France and the French. I just loved being in Paris – well-dressed people effortlessly speaking French (how did they manage that?), actually sitting outside cafés, riding the Metro, exhaling stale garlic and Gauloises fumes, drinking red wine and wearing fashionable clothes. I had seen pictures in books and even the odd French film, but suddenly this was the real thing. Marianne made Britannia seem rather boring.

Though we hardly realised it at the time, we were lucky the trip had been organised by our two French teachers, who were only a few years older than us, belonging to the post-war generation of graduate teachers, often in conflict with their older colleagues. Imagine our delight in finding we were not living in some Lycée dormitory, but in a faintly louche small hotel near Place Pigalle, and dining not in a student refectory but in a famous restaurant next door to the Moulin Rouge. Imagine too the edgy treat of real (but sadly static) near-naked young women on stage; I for one was acutely aware of being in the company of school friends and teachers. I am convinced that our headmaster knew nothing of this avant-garde approach to secondary education.

I suspect also that this trip was a not-so-subtle ploy to tempt some of us to take French in the sixth form and maybe go on to study it at University. In my case I was only too pleased to oblige.

Because of my abject failures at O-level, I assumed that I would be out on my ear, but for reasons I still don't fully understand, I was invited to stay on in the sixth form to take an arts-based A-level course. I rather suspect that the headmaster's limited grasp of educational realities had led to a depleted sixth form, which didn't reflect well on the school, so the normal entrance bar may have been discreetly lowered. I also think that one or two teachers had spotted in me some aptitude for arts subjects and thought I deserved a second chance. Whatever, it was an offer I could hardly refuse.

Entry into the sixth form came with some attractive benefits. The horrible brown and yellow uniform was replaced by slightly less revolting piping-less black blazer and smart grey trousers for the boys, knee-length skirts for the girls. No miniskirts then. We had our own base-room where we could hang out when not in class. We could make our own hot drinks and eat our lunch in our base-room, away from the dreaded school dinner hall. Games were optional, much to the chagrin of Probert the rugby. This was the revolution, on the cusp of the swinging sixties, treating us almost like grown-ups. Real bonds of friendship (and even romances,) were formed between sixth-formers who hardly knew each other. As far as I know, none of them came from our prefab estate.

I look back on this time as one of the most formative of my life.

My brother Charlie had quite a different big school experience. He failed his eleven plus and went to the nearest secondary modern, Millers Way. He didn't give a hoot. I had a brown uniform, his was maroon, so what. As far as I could tell, he had a whale of a time, unencumbered by boring academic learning.

Until recently I had little idea of what he got up to at school. Though our two schools were quite near each other, they seemed a world apart. Charlie wasn't particularly interested in my day-to-day school life, and I could never get him to tell me much about his. I knew he had girlfriends, went out to ice hockey matches, hung out with his mates on the estate, played guitar in a skiffle group and spent a lot of his spare time next door with Mary, who went to a different grammar school. He loved helping Mum at home and often took over the role of cook, trying out new recipes he'd learned at the secondary modern, where boys could sign up for domestic science lessons. He always seemed happy with his life, and he was popular. I think the eleven plus system made it easy for us to drift further and further apart, even though we had been inseparable as young children and still lived in the same small house.

Chapter 16 | Never a dull moment

1970

He is lost in the city he knows so well. His shift is over, and all he has to do is to find the station, but somehow it's not where it should be. He has the feeling this has happened before, but the more he tries to retrace his steps, the more he knows he will never find his way home. At each junction his sense of direction tells him which way to go, but he no longer recognises these streets. Then suddenly he knows what is round the next corner. He is no longer in a city street, but clambering over dunes, heading for the sea. It seems quite normal. A young woman passes by and smiles at him. She seems somehow familiar, but he has forgotten her name. As she disappears, he understands that it's not so far from central London to the seaside after all. He's turned south, that's all. Could be worse, but Olive and the boys will be worried.

Then he hears a dog bark. It can't be Mathilda, she died years ago.

Bugger. No dunes, no girl, no sound of distant waves. Just the familiar prefab bedroom, and the black cloud that has been hanging over them for months. Sod it. The final notice to quit threatens from his bedside table, together with a copy of the rehousing agreement, signed by them both. Confirming the end of their tenancy and their way of life. In two weeks' time their prefab home will be demolished, only twelve years late. They don't want a new life. Nothing wrong with the old one. Why can't they just be left alone, in peace?

So much for his Sunday lie-in, alone in the marital bed they have shared since they moved into number 35. Olive is at Church. When did she start going to church? Why, for that matter?

The planning department's decision is not unexpected. Friars Walk tenants have been fighting a two-year long campaign to save their homes, which they love so dearly. The tenants' association were no help. Harry and Bill argued that the prefabs were as sound as the day they were bolted together in 1947. They saw no reason to bring in the bulldozers, other than snobbery and suspected vested interests. As residents, they have paid their rents and rates like anyone else, and they still feel they have a right to stay put if they wish. The council has argued that the prefabs are sub-standard now and all residents can be rehoused in nicer, warmer, brick-built housing not far away. Flats of course.

'Bloody town planners – stuck up bastards – what do they know about decent working people anyway? Or even care? Brilliant timing as usual too. Is this what we fought for? If only.....'

Now the dreaded corrosion card has been played. Game over. In any case, the resistance campaign has fizzled out as one by one most of their neighbours caved in. Some have moved into the first flats built on the new estate, others have just packed up and disappeared. All except Harry and Olive, Bill and Agnes. Two forlorn prefabs side-by-side, worth their weight in aluminium, identical twins stranded in the overgrown brown-field site now destined to become a shiny new shopping parade. The bulldozers are circling. Keeping them awake at night. Arc lamps left on overnight. Threatening. Under orders no doubt.

Harry can't get all this out of his head. They have lived at number 35 ever the since the prefabs were assembled on site in the cruel winter of '46-47, before the road was built. Now, as the last sitting tenants, they are defeated by corroded window frames. Why can't they just fit new frames? Why enforce eviction? Well, rehousing anyway. This is where they have brought up their kids, tended their garden, papered the walls, paid their way, tried to get along with all and sundry, made friends and enemies, some for life. Their kids are doing well too. Tom teaching at the comprehensive that has replaced the grammar school he went to, and Charlie, now doing so well in New Zealand. Mary next door now developing vaccines in America.

The ghosts of the friars have bowed their shaven heads and shuffled away.

The front door clicks, interrupting Harry's thoughts, just as he was getting up steam.

'Hallo?'

'It's only me darling. Are you up?'

'Didn't realise it was so late……'

'Lazy man!'

'I confess.'

'Get dressed.'

Padding out to the kitchen in his dressing gown to make the coffee, still wallowing in self-pity and pointless anger, Harry is interrupted by a well-known knock at the side door.

'Bugger.'

He groans. It's their chirpy chappie neighbour Electric Bill. Only he knocks to the rhythm of the Skye boat song.

'What ho misery-guts, up at last! Is that coffee I smell? See, I only come round when that fair lady of yours is in. Don't understand what she sees in you, personally.'

'Leave it out Bill for once in your life. Okay, coffee it is, if it shuts you up.' Fat chance.

Bill, ever the bright spark (ho ho), breezes in and takes his usual kitchen chair. Harry, Olive, Bill and Agnes met the day their families moved in. To say they had always been close friends would be an exaggeration. More like fond toleration. You didn't get to choose your neighbours. The two women get on fine, but the men never are that close. For Harry, Bill is more like an extra brother, one who goes home next door when things get rough, unlike his own irritating brothers when he was growing up.

'Working on a Sunday then? You wouldn't get away with that where you come from. The Lord would have you struck down on the spot. No wonder you're loaded.'

'Aye, double bubble. It's those new builds over at North Road. Mains sockets have failed the tests and tenants are supposed to be in by next week. So you two have signed up then?

'Yes. Let's face it, no choice really, we've been clutching at straws long enough. Corrosion indeed. If it's true it's their own fault for lack of maintenance. Just an excuse. Olive's still dead against living in a flat – she'll miss the garden and she'll not be so good climbing all those stairs, with her back. She reckons we'll be kept awake by noisy neighbours too. She could be right. At least we'll be nearer the shops in the new place. And the station. This time next year there'll be a Woolworths right here. OK if you like Pick n Mix I suppose. We've talked it over with the boys and they both feel for us. They must have some fond memories of growing up here. Tom has always thought we should have moved ten years ago.'

'Well, you already know we've signed up. Never mind all the bullshit the council are peddling; I've had a peek at the specs for the new flats. Don't ask how. I must admit, they're the bee's knees mate, and no mistake. Fitted kitchens, two or three beds, gas central heating, quiet cul-de-sac, garage blocks – the works. We tried our best mate, but…..'

Suddenly Olive storms into the kitchen. Followed by a tall man, complete with clipboard, himself followed by three more blokes lugging black boxes up the path from a van parked outside. It says BBC on the side.

'What the dickens have you been up to now Harry Dobson? This bloke says he's from the BBC. Nobody told me.'

Harry is taken aback. 'Ah, sorry dear, it's just an interview for Nationwide. Slipped my mind.'

'Liar. I bet this is something to do with your stupid resistance brigade. Or what's left of it. What's the point? It's over. Why can't you accept it? You and your bloody politics…..'

'It's not about my politics, it's about a crooked Tory council lining their pockets. Treating loyal tenants like trash. Outrageous if you ask me…..'

'Nobody's asking you anymore. It's all in your head Harry. All in your stupid head. Still playing the local hero, but nobody's interested. I thought we'd agreed to go quietly so we could get the best deal on a new house?'

'And we will get a good deal dear, they won't dare go back on their promises after they get grilled on the telly.'

The tall man from the BBC is fascinated. Adjusting his brand-new black horn-rimmed glasses, his journo brain cells buzz. More in this story than he'd thought.

'Um, sorry to butt in, but I'm not here to grill anybody, and we don't want to upset you Mrs Dobson. If you'd like to talk in private, we can wait outside'.

Harry smiles. 'Yes, sorry. Give us a few minutes.'

'OK. My name is Jonathan by the way. I'll wait in the car Mr Dobson.'

After he leaves Olive has tears in her eyes. She rarely cries.

'Oh, do what you want. Why break the habit of a lifetime. Why do I bother? Just one thing – I'm not having all that clutter in here. You'll have to do it outside. And don't think I want to be on the telly, not like some round here. And I don't want everyone to see inside our house.'

Olive leaves for the bedroom, taking care not to bang the door behind her. More threatening that way. Silence descends. Jonathan and the crew leave by the front door and walk down the concrete path. He looks up at the threatening sky and shrugs. The clock in the front room ticks. It was a wedding present from Olive's brother. It seems louder than usual.

Time for Electric Bill to chip in. 'Bloody hell Harry. You've done it this time. Fame at last.'

'Well I never thought they'd turn up today. I was going to break it gently to Olive. He said they would call me beforehand. Obviously forgotten we don't have a phone. I didn't know the BBC worked Sundays. Bet they're on double bubble too'.

'Doghouse for you I reckon. I'm out of here mate'.

'Oh no you don't, you weasel. I'm going to need you. You can share the bloody fame.'

'You mean you're going through with it? Olive's right, you're an idiot. An obstinate idiot at that.'

'Don't let me down Bill. I can't do this on my own – you can't desert me now, after all we've done together. Olive will come round, she always does. I'll tell the man. What's his name again?'

'Jonathan.'

As she changes out of her Sunday best in their bedroom, Olive tries to calm herself, as she has a thousand times. No Sunday dinner for you today. Lucky if you get a fish-paste sandwich. More than you deserve. If only her Charlie had not left home. He'd have sorted this out all right. Told the BBC where to get off. Nationwide indeed, what next?

Chapter 17 | Expanding the horizons

Transcript: Episode 9 of a series of podcasts recorded during the third Covid-19 lockdown, 2021. Written and read by Tom Dobson.

1958 / 1959

In my teens, my liberation from the confines of life in NW13 was my bike – a Triumph Palm Beach 3 speed tourer. This wonderful bike was my escape machine, on which I used to explore the home counties, Hertfordshire and Buckinghamshire, to travel to my Auntie's place, or to spend the summer holidays on long distance youth hostelling jaunts.

I think I was fourteen when I finally got the bike. For ages I had been lobbying for one, mainly on the reasonable grounds that everyone else had one, but my Dad was adamant, on equally reasonable grounds, that I would not last five minutes on busy streets. As a result, by the time I did get my way, I had missed out on a few years of practice on the road, compared to other kids on the patch. I can't remember anyone teaching me to ride.

My parents could not afford the outlay back then, but I managed to save up at least part of the cost from what I earned in various Saturday jobs. Looking back, I can't understand why the bike had to be brand new. All I had to go on was what I could see in the local bike shops. Or did it have something to do with keeping up with my peers, as a working-class boy in a grammar school? Some of my classmates had racers, with drop handlebars and derailleur gears, but I went off that idea when I found out how much they cost, and after a friend went over his handlebars one day and broke his jaw. He had to spend months with his upper and lower teeth cemented together, sucking up soup though a straw and having the mickey taken by his younger brothers.

I dread to think now how I managed to survive my first forays out into outer Metroland. I must have become over-confident when I had my one-and-only accident, about five miles from home. Nobody was around at the time, which was both good and bad news. Good because I felt so stupid – it was totally my own carelessness that made me come off the bike – bad because my foot got entangled with the front wheel, which hurt. I ended up with a few bruises, a sprained ankle and bike with a bent wheel. I tried pushing the bike home but soon realised that wasn't going to work, so I stopped at a phone box and called my auntie who lived about ten miles away. Uncle Fred to the rescue! Good job he had a car.

The aftermath was even worse. The humiliation I felt was acute, especially after my dad's dire warnings, and the bike was useless now. I can't recall who paid for the repair or how long it took, but in due course I was back in the saddle, if not wiser at least a little more cautious. I was lucky – no helmets or mobile phones in those days.

Once back on the road, I spent most of my weekends touring alone in the countryside, with only a road map to guide me, a pack-up for sustenance and pocket-money for the occasional Mars bar. I rarely travel those roads now, but I can still see those signs pointing to Amersham, Radlett, Princes Risborough or Ivinghoe, and I recall those home county high streets, village greens, high hedges and tea shops.

The next step in the liberation master plan was to join the Youth Hostels Association, that wonderful self-help organization which did so much for young people (and sometimes not-so-young people), enabling us to roam not just in Britain but around the world. I gather the rules have changed since those days, but the bottom lines then were single-sex dormitories, no motorised transport and a duty to work for your keep. There was also a sense of belonging, but without any compulsion to fit into an ethos. I had tried the wolf cubs and the church. I was put off cubs when one of them told me that among the alleged benefits was that you could boil live tadpoles, and as for the church, I just found it all hard to believe, though I did quite like singing hymns, and there were some nice girls too of a Sunday. These were short-lived attempts to expand my horizons, but the YHA lasted a bit longer. I was beginning to see myself as a bit of a loner, the open road before me, the prefab estate left far behind.

I had become friendly with Daniel, a curate's son who had a rather sedate gearless touring bike. I can't remember the make, but I do remember the brakes worked by peddling backwards. I tried it out once and nearly went over the handlebars.

Daniel's mum was a lovely woman. She used to provide tea and cakes at their house when we bunked off cross country running once a week. Daniel's home life was so different from mine – he read music, sang in the church choir, played the organ and piano and was top of the class at Canonsbury grammar school. He was interested in churches and cathedrals, so we cooked up a plan to spend our summer holidays going on a bike tour of English cathedral towns, staying in youth hostels. Hard to believe now, but we pulled it off.

I think my Palm Beach was really classified as a city bike, but I seem to remember that we planned our tour so we never had more than thirty miles between overnights – modest compared to today's mileages made possible by lighter bikes and derailleur gears. We also avoided A roads as much as possible and had frequent rest stops along the way. It doesn't sound like much now I suppose, but I can truly say this experience changed my life. Looking back, the hostelling experience alone was an education, and the adventure inspired in me a love of the countryside, an appreciation of fine buildings and the sheer thrill of self-reliance.

Our circular tour took us south from NW13, via Southwark, Winchester, Exeter, Wells, Gloucester and Worcester cathedrals. My memory is hazy about other towns and villages we visited on the way. I'm equally unsure of the total mileage, but I think we were on the road for at least a month, so let's say at least 600 miles come rain or shine, and there was plenty of both. Not bad for a couple of oddballs on unsuitable bikes. And off them when need be.

There was a sequel to our tour. Daniel studied German at school and had joined up to a student exchange scheme. The trouble was that his exchange pairing was with identical twin boys. Rather reluctantly I agreed to accompany him on a visit to stay with them in Stuttgart, making up the numbers.

We had absolutely nothing in common with the twins. The family was evidently rich. For a start they lived in an enormous modern house on the outskirts of Stuttgart, occupied by the family, two dependent female relatives and another family who rented the ground floor. Their father, an eccentric architect, ran his own business in the basement.

We had travelled by train to Stuttgart, before being driven to this family home in Bad Cannstatt. We were shattered but had to sit down to the biggest supper I had ever seen other than in the movies. It came with beer and wine too, so I went to bed that night sozzled. Because I didn't do German at school I found this hard going, and I was totally dependent on Daniel. It was only too evident that the muscle-bound twins were not the slightest bit interested in us pallid specimens of English youth. It didn't take long to realise that this exchange was a mutually pointless exercise cooked up by well-intentioned adults who wanted to transform recent enemies into friends. From the moment we arrived, the twins just ignored us, which suited me fine.

Mostly I missed my bike, but we were totally spoilt by Frau Gerber. The daily routine was huge breakfast, walk, huge lunch, free time, huge alcoholic supper, TV, bed. We managed to find the bus into Stuttgart, and we were taken to an enormous Mercedes engine factory, then invited to spend an amazing day with Herr Gerber when he drove to Bavaria, ostensibly to inspect progress on various opulent country houses for rich clients. He drove like a maniac, bouncing around through country lanes and farmyards, getting lost several times. Every time the Mercedes went over a bump at speed, which was all the time, the horn would go off, scaring us, passers-by and numerous chickens. Some kind of loose connection apparently. Under the bonnet, he explained to Daniel. In his brain, I thought.

I couldn't help liking this bloke though, even if he had been a major or something in the war. Later, I did wonder how he had made all his money, and how his clients must have made theirs. The high point of this trip was lunch, taken in a vast restaurant high up in the Bavarian hills. They specialized in fresh trout. They couldn't have been fresher. You chose your fish from a shoal swimming happily in a glass tank in the centre of the room, never expecting its end was nigh. Herr Grimm ordered chips and booze. When the chips came, they were served on a platter the size of a dustbin lid.

Herr Grimm supported an unmarried sister and his aged mother, who lived on the top floor. They never appeared on the family floor, but Frau Grimm explained that she cooked for them and they paid for a servant to come in to look after them. I don't remember the sister, but the old lady was wonderful. She used to accost us on the stairs, smiling, hugging and talking nineteen to the dozen. Even Daniel was bamboozled, so we just did a lot of smiling and nodding. It turned out that she was speaking Schwäbisch, her original German dialect. The only verb I came to recognise was *spaziergang machen* which means to go for a walk. It made sense - we did little else, other than ride buses, stuff ourselves and get tipsy.

We saw the twins only at mealtimes, and communication was impossible. Their main interests, apart from ignoring us, seemed to be tennis, themselves, and girls. Preferably at the same times. We never saw the girls.

The trip was not a total disaster, but there was worse to come. Far worse.

A year later, when it was their turn to come to England it was decided that the twins would bring along very impressive Teutonic bikes, bought for the occasion, so that they could come with us on a second cathedral city tour. They hadn't changed, and nor had we. Don't blame me, it wasn't my idea.

Cathedrals were far from their twin minds. Their idea of cycling was to race each other and scare the natives with these weird sirens they had, powered by the wheels. They wanted to go to Heathrow, just to try them out in the tunnel, pedalling as fast as their tennis-trained legs could propel them. After the fourth run, they were removed by a very irritated police patrol. We disowned them.

The tour itself was a disaster, punctuated by screams in the night uttered by one of them, and ending in their arrest under suspicion of spying on a naval base somewhere on the south coast. More police, military this time. The cops phoned Daniel's mum to verify our story. The next day we saw the twins off on the train with a sigh of relief and never saw them or their family again. Daniel and I finished the tour, in our plodding way, but somehow the incident had taken the shine off touring. We never did it again.

By the way, it seems fitting to shout three cheers for Triumph bikes and the Sturmey Archer hub gearbox, originally invented by Henry Sturmey in 1902. The rich history of the world's first 3-speed internal gear hub for bicycles began in Nottingham, when it transformed city bike riding. For me, the beauty of the hub gearbox was that your drive chain didn't come off when you least expected it. On the other hand, if it went wrong you could be in for an expensive repair or replacement. Mine never went wrong.

I reluctantly sold the Palm Beach after I left full-time occupation of the prefab, for university. A mistake, with hindsight. I like to think someone else got a second life out of her anyway. I have only seen one since, quite recently, chained up to the railings outside a city railway station. It belonged to one of the staff, who had been riding it to and from work for over 40 years.

Chapter 18 | Fame at last

1970

The tall young man from the BBC, Nationwide reporter Jonathan Fairchild, is dressed in a style that suggests an assignment in the rain forests of Brazil rather than a dull English suburb. Safari-type jacket, light cotton trousers, tan brogues. Mercifully no toupee. Somewhat deflated by Olive's introduction he feels he must assert some degree of authority after the dodgy start at prefab number thirty-five. After all, he is a BBC man, nephew of the pioneer radio broadcaster and wartime hero Gough Wilson. Back in the front room he addresses Harry, the punter he has come to interview about the battle of Friars Walk:

'Sorry Mr Dobson, we tried to call you, but nobody told me you don't have a phone. We don't usually come out to play on Sundays, but a little bird told me the bulldozers will be back any day now, and it only makes sense to do this while the last two prefabs are still standing. Do call me Jonny (no aitch by the way).'

Harry, still in his pyjamas, dressing gown and carpet slippers, is trying hard to get his act together. 'Er, yes, of course. Sorry about the phone thing. The estate's never been wired up. Everyone uses the phone box on the main road. Bloody nuisance that, standing in all weathers and pumping coins. I suppose they never thought the likes of us would need our own phones. Now, do you want to do this on the street or in the garden or what?

'Well, both if possible, and maybe round what's left of the estate?'

'Ok Jonny. Garden it is. I guess you'll need permission from the council to film on the building site…..'

'Leave that to us Harry.'

'Right, I'll just get dressed and have a quick wash. Can Bill chip in? He and Agnes are in the same boat. We're a team really. '

'No problem.'

During this conversation, one of the crew, evidently the cameraman, has been sizing up the front room. He's not up with the game.

'Jonny, a word. Might be best to do this outdoors if possible, one way and another. Not much room to set up indoors, and we would need to bring in at least two redheads.'

Redheads? Redheads? Tom and Bill are gobsmacked. Dancing girls next?

'Well we can't shoot indoors anyway, so that's no problem. Sorry, I should have said.' Jonny replies.

'Harry, Bill, this is Alex, our brilliant cameraman. To translate, Redheads are powerful mains lights, and would hold us up. We're not sure your mains supply would have taken the load either. It's shame we can't see indoors, but I understand why.'

Cue Bill. 'What you need is an electrician. It just happens that I......'

Harry cuts him off. 'Bill! At least it's not raining or snowing.'

Another crew member pipes up. It's Jim, the sound man. 'Not too much wind either boss, so sound should not too problematic. You're in luck today. Can we set up in the back garden? Less road noise, I hope.'

So while Harry gets dressed and Olive refuses to talk to him, the BBC crew get to work, taking all their gear round the back, without tramping through the prefab. Bill seems fascinated with the technicalities, though he has the sense not to ask questions as the camera and sound gear are unpacked from their flight cases and assembled in the back garden. Olive decides she'll be better off next door with Agnes and Mary, who's home for a break.

Harry's relieved. Agnes is a good calmer-down. The doghouse is looking like an understatement. Divorce more like.

When Harry reappears, sporting his only suit and cravat, Jonny talks to him and Bill in the kitchen, together with an attractive young lady, recently arrived by car, who takes notes. She is introduced as their equally brilliant production assistant Mandy. Her brilliance is evidenced mainly by a mini-skirt, long dark hair, another clipboard, a stopwatch, one of those clapper board contraptions clasped to an ample bosom, and a cheery demeanour. Bill finds it hard to keep his eyes off her, but she's used to that.

Jonathan speaks up. 'Let's just recap, folks. The angle I have in mind is that though prefabs have a bad reputation, they are cherished by those who live in them. I expect you both to have strong views about that. From my research, I gather that people like you love your prefabs, and you resent being kicked out. Right?'

'Spot on Jonny, but can we say other things?' Harry asks.

'Of course, but one or two things to take on board. Best not to rant or swear – it's not in your interest. We can't broadcast anything defamatory, so don't make negative allegations about anyone else, and don't name names, however strongly you feel. I know you are mad at the council, but unless you have evidence, we would have to cut those bits out anyway. OK? Any questions?'

'Yes. When will it be on?' Bill asks.

'Well I can't be sure. Probably sometime next week. It's quite normal on Nationwide for the running order not to be fixed on any day, right up to transmission, and sometimes it changes while the programme is on air. I'll do my best to ring you when I know more. Oh, no - no phone. We'll send a telegram or a runner. If the bulldozers do move in tomorrow or Tuesday we might send a stringer to film that too, and that could delay transmission further.'

Harry's now raring to go. 'Clear enough. Let's know when you want us outside.'

'Hang on then, any moment now – I'll check.'

While Jonny is out of the room, Bill and Harry exchange nervous grins.

'What the hell's a stringer, do you reckon?'

'Buggered if I know Bill.'

'Plenty of gobbledygook, this bloke, and no mistake. I rather fancy that.....'

'Shut up Bill, you're a married man, and Agnes is not daft. That Mandy would have you for breakfast anyway. And watch your step. No lip on camera.'

Jonny reappears and gives a double thumbs up. In the garden Alex has set up the camera and he tells them where to stand. Jim, now sporting some impressive headphones, asks them each in turn to say a few words so he can set the sound levels, aided by Jonathan who now has a microphone disguised as something resembling a dead cat.

'Happy everyone?' Nods all round.

'Turn over please...........?'

Alex gives the thumbs-up, Jim nods and Jonny asks the first question.

Interview Transcript, as logged by Mandy Walker:

Jonny: Harry, do you actually like living in a prefab?'

Harry: Of course, why not? We don't just like living here, we love it. It's not a prison sentence. We'd hardly have stayed here since 1947 if we didn't like it, would we? When we moved in we were told the prefabs would only be temporary, Churchill's quick fix to the post-war housing crisis. The problem now is estates like this have lasted so much longer, lulling people like us residents into a state of false security.

Jonny: So why are they pulling them down now do you think?

Harry: Complicated. I think it's a combination of factors. The first would be money. Economics trump humanity these days. Our prefabs have lasted so long because we have maintained them so well ourselves, but even so the costs to the council keep going up, so they're losing money. Then there's a land use issue. The council are going to make a packet out of this, even though they have to pay for us to be rehoused. This place will disappear in the next few days because our rents don't make the kind of profits they have already made when they sold the land off to the developers and gave permission to build the new shopping parade. I also think it's about class and snobbery. Right

116

from the start, homeowners in this country have looked down on council houses, especially prefabs and the decent people who live in them. I didn't realise it at first, but prefab estates are regarded as slums by stuck up homeowners and the like.

Jonny: Do you agree Bill?

Bill: I certainly do my friend. In my job as an electrician I have been inside thousands of homes, so I have seen all kinds of places, warts and all. Believe me, you couldn't make it up. Just because you own your own house doesn't mean it's a palace. Older houses are usually damp, with leaky gas and dodgy electrics, postage stamp back yards instead of gardens like this one, and poor sanitation. Prefab folks look after their homes. They take pride in them. I have never been inside a prefab, or any other council house, which was allowed to become dangerous or not fit to live in, so they're talking utter rubbish, these people. I think it's envy. Most of them have never been on a prefab estate, so their view is worthless in my opinion. We had no choice about who lived where, but this used to be a real community. We looked out for each other. Not like now when folks don't know or care about their neighbours.

Harry: To blazes with them – I reckon that lot of people who had bought their own houses were jealous when ex-servicemen and their families got brand new all-electric homes to bring up a new generation. The best people to ask about prefab life are the kids who were brought up here. As far as I know, they all say the same, it was the best time of their life. I would invite your viewers here anytime, with pride. Pity we won't be here much longer of course.

Jonny: Thanks to you both. Hope you enjoy your new homes............Cut!

As Alex turns the camera off Harry and Bill hear applause. Agnes, Mary and Olive have been following the interview over the fence, out of shot, accompanied by a small group of friends who have somehow cottoned on. Harry and Bill take a bow. Harry is surprised to see that his son Tom is there too, clapping and smiling. When he catches his father's eye, he gives the thumbs up. The BBC crew are smiling too. Fame at last.

Later that evening, the two couples celebrate with Tom, who usually drops round for Sunday dinner. Mary has come over too, once she realised Tom was home. Olive has come round a bit. She and Agnes are a bit tipsy.

Olive gets in first: 'I didn't know you could talk like that,

either of you.'

'Nor did we, duck.' Harry responds.

'Hands up, I thought you two were going to be a disaster

and I'd never live it down.'

That night, in bed Olive sleeps soundly, as if the day has been just like any other, but Harry can't drop off. The events of the day just won't go away. He knows all the tricks, but they don't always work. Eventually his mind turns back to the woman in his dream that morning. He shops around in his memories and finally realises who she was, and where he had ended up on his way to the station. She was the niece of the elderly couple he had been billeted with near Bayeux after D-Day. He once went with the family to picnic, and she had tried to teach him some basic French. He wonders if she dreams about him.

Chapter 19 | Music for a while

<u>Transcript: Episode 10 of a series of podcasts recorded during the third Covid-19 lockdown, 2021. Written and read by Tom Dobson.</u>

<u>1947 - 2021</u>

As teenagers, Charlie and I had divergent tastes in music. Charlie liked pop songs, and when he was at Millers Way secondary modern, he joined a skiffle group, inspired by Lonnie Donegan. I made his first guitar at home and in the woodwork room at Canonsbury High. We had little access to music at home because all we had was the one wireless set, in the front room. Dad used to listen to classical music on the BBC third programme when we had gone to bed. I'm not sure about mum's musical tastes, but I think she shared her sisters' liking for popular dance music and sentimental ballads. Something with a tune. Some kids went for music lessons, piano or violin, but it was never on offer for us.

I must have been ten years old when I noticed a mandolin in a junk shop window. It was filthy, with tarnished strings. I had read about the mandolin in a library book about musical instruments. I knew they had four double strings, normally tuned like the violin, GDAE, and that they were usually made in Naples. I also learnt that they were played with a plectrum, like some guitars. I think I had also heard Vivaldi's mandolin concerto on the wireless.

I had somehow saved up a pound, but I had no idea how much the mandolin in the window would cost. There was a price tag tied to a tuning peg, but I couldn't read it because it faced inward. I dared not go inside the shop on my own, so I asked mum if she would come with me to have a closer look. I expected her to put me off, but she seemed oddly interested in the idea, and a few days later, on a grey rainy day, we took the bus to the small row of shops which included the junk shop. I was fearful that it might have been sold or that I couldn't afford it, or the shop might be closed. But there it was, partly obscured by an ugly vase. There was a faint glimmer of a light somewhere in the shop. Mum seemed as nervous as I was.

When mum pushed the door open, a bell rang. A few minutes later a young man sporting a checked waistcoat appeared and invited mum to look round. Had we anything in particular in mind? Yes, my son would like to have a look at that mandolin in the window. Minutes later, after the twanging mandolin had been carefully extricated from the tightly packed shop window, I had the dusty instrument in my hands. Mum asked if I could strum the strings. It sounded terrible, but mum pointed out that it would need to be restrung and tuned. I was impressed - she sounded remarkably well-informed. She took the mandolin from me and immediately had a go at tuning it up by ear. She played a chord, fiddled with the tuning again, then played a tune she liked, humming as she picked out the melody. Oh, My Darling Clementine. The salesman's face lit up. Rooted to the spot, I realised my mouth was open. Obviously, there was something I had not been told about my mum. She knew the words too, so she and the salesman sang along, much to my embarrassment.

Oh my darling, oh my darling
Oh my darling, Clementine
You were lost and gone forever
Dreadful sorrow, Clementine
In a cavern, in a canyon
Excavating for a mine
Dwelt a miner forty-niner
And his daughter, Clementine

And so on..........

Even its poor state of repair, the mandolin sounded quite good, but by then we had noticed the price on the tag was twenty-five shillings, so my pound was not enough. I was desperate. How could I get the extra five shillings? Let alone the cost of new strings. Mum asked if the instrument could be reserved until I saved up the balance. The salesman sadly shook his head, but he was smiling at mum. As we turned to go, he asked her if she came from Norfolk by any chance. He'd picked up her now faint accent. Mum said yes, she came from Acle. He came from Norwich. I knew flirting when I witnessed it. The price was reduced to a pound, and the deal was done. Make sure he learns to play like you, he said, as we left with the prize in mum's shopping bag, zipped up against the drizzle.

I didn't ask mum how she knew how to play the mandolin, or why she'd never mentioned it, but years later she told me that as a teenager she had borrowed one from somebody in her village and had taught herself to play popular tunes by ear. Mandolins were very poplar when she was a girl, and there was even a craze for mandolin bands and orchestras. She said this was our secret. Dad doesn't know.

When I got it home, I carefully cleaned the mandolin up, removing years of grime, using turpentine and furniture polish, as advised by Uncle Albert. This revealed its beauty – the mellow sheen of the sounding board, the twinkle of inlaid mother of pearl around the sound hole, the deep tones of the neck, bowl and head, the black surface of the ebony fretboard and bridge, the creamy ivory tuning buttons and nut. The strings weren't as bad as we thought, just tarnished, so I just buffed them up with Brasso. I got by with an improvised plastic plectrum until Uncle Albert donated a set of tortoiseshell ones. He also bought me a tuning fork and mum taught me how to tune the instrument with it, using the seventh frets.

However, what I needed then was a teacher, and that was out of the question, so my lovely mandolin, made by the Neapolitan Pietro Tonelli in Naples, became a beautiful wall ornament. It had a brief revival years later when mum had it restrung and Charlie learned to play it for his folk group, as an alternative to the guitar I made for him. Like mum, he had the knack, and I was happy for him. His girlfriend Chiara was Italian, but she had never heard of mandolins, which surprised me. Anyway, she preferred the guitar because it was easier to learn and play chords.

After half a lifetime hanging on various walls, my old mandolin has recently staged a comeback. Unfinished business. Something to do in retirement, I thought. On impulse I set myself the task of mastering the instrument, with some initial success. But mandolins had changed. The Tonelli was all but unplayable, so back on the wall it went, where it remains today, in honourable retirement itself. No strings or bridge now, the soundboard cracked beyond repair. Undeterred, I bought a second-hand modern flat-back mandolin and painstakingly I have taught myself to play folk tunes, by ear, copying from CDs and YouTube videos. I went to some summer schools and joined a local folk group for a while. To my joy I found I could jam along, even when the song was new to me. Now I have a modest repertoire to embarrass people with.

When my dad died, I realised I may have underestimated his love of classical music. I discovered hundreds of audio cassettes, recorded off-air from the third programme, carefully packed in shoe boxes, stored in the shed. Mostly the romantics, Beethoven, Tchaikovsky, Mahler. He must have collected these after Charlie and I left home.

Not long after we moved into the prefab, out of the blue, we had acquired a radiogram, donated by a lady mum used to work for as a cleaner. This impressive piece of furniture comprised a shiny veneered art deco cabinet with a wind-up record player upstairs, a radio downstairs and a loudspeaker at the front. You needed lots of steel needles, and a supply of 78rpm ten or twelve-inch shellac discs. I did manage to buy a few sixpenny discs from junk shops, more or less at random, but sooner or later they either wore out or got broken.

Canonsbury had no school orchestra, but a quite successful choir. I joined as a boy alto, but like many another I had to give it up when my voice broke. The repertoire was pretty standard, the Messiah, Bach's Mass in b Minor, The Creation. Good fun while it lasted, and a great way to find a girlfriend. At school I was never taught to read music, nor to play a musical instrument properly.

Neither of these disadvantages prevented me from clambering aboard a battered coach one day, heading for the BBC's Maida Vale studios, to sing for schools' radio, along with a small group of singers selected by audition. The radio series was the very same one I had been subjected to weekly at primary school, where a school choir would sing a song or two for other schools, listening in throughout the nation. Live.

I didn't think for a moment I would survive the audition. For a start we were not supposed to know what songs we would be singing, and I lied when I said I could read music. But somehow, the identity of the songs had been leaked before the auditions, possibly by our music teacher, and we sang each of them in class beforehand, so I learned them by heart and pretended I was following the score. I don't think I fooled anyone, but anyway I got picked.

On the big day, when the red transmission light went on in the cavernous recording studio, a man with a posh voice introduced us as the choir of Canonsbury Grammar School, and off we went, singing Me and Molly Maloney and Sir Englamour. On the way back, a friend of mine was sick in the bus. Little did we know then that the Maida Vale studios would become famous, with artists and groups like Led Zeppelin and The Beatles recording and transmitting for various BBC radio shows, including the John Peel sessions.

My first sustained introduction to classical music came about through my friendship with my classmate, Daniel, the curate's son, who had the advantage of a musical education. We went to early music concerts in London. I liked what I heard - Bach, Purcell, Handel, Dowland, Palestrina, Byrd, Taverner, Gibbons. Daniel occasionally played on Handel's organ at St. Lawrence Whitchurch. This was a whole new world for me. We went to services at St. Paul's Cathedral to hear Alfred Deller, the famous counter tenor, who was Daniel's idol. The fact that I had rejected Christianity made no difference, I just loved the sound of this music and the thrill of discovery.

By the late-fifties, most families on the estate seemed to have a record player, and some kids even had their own Dansette in their bedroom, capable of playing singles, EPs and LP albums. Dad just wouldn't have one in the house, even though he could have enjoyed building his own collection of symphonic music if he had. Charlie solved the problem by going round to his friends' prefabs, but I was determined to have a record player of my own, or even a tape recorder.

I was already interested in electrics and electronics, and with a bit of help from Practical Wireless magazine, Electric Bill next door and two uncles, I had managed to build a radio and a mono amplifier. I became a denizen of surplus electronic supplies, raiding shops in Tottenham Court Road and the Edgware Road, scooping up valves, resistors, transformers, plugs, sockets, loudspeakers and capacitors, right, left and centre. I simply followed the instructions and wiring diagrams published in Practical Wireless. My Uncle Albert gave me a soldering iron and taught me how to use it.

After some infuriating failures, I eventually constructed a working record player in my half of the back bedroom. The problem was how to house it. The immediate solution was to disembowel the old radiogram and fit it out with a deck and new all-electronic guts. After the usual teething problems, this worked fine, but because of its bulk, it could only sit in the living room, whereas the objective was to have a record player in the back bedroom so that Charlie and I could entertain ourselves independently. So I installed the deck and amplifier, along with a smaller speaker, in a much smaller cube-shaped cabinet which I built out of plywood and covered with Rexine. This worked well, until the stereo era began. By the time transistors replaced valves and Charlie went to sea, my mission was accomplished, and music rang out daily in the back bedroom of the prefab.

Now that I had a record player, albeit home-made, and despite a lack of funds, I could move on. We still listened to the radio, so when I heard a piece of music I might one day want to buy, I would write down the details. The only snag was when the music was not identified on air. One instance was the theme tune to a home-service thriller called Counterspy. It was a major emotional jolt. I became obsessed by these few bars of the most exciting music I had ever heard, so I wrote to the

BBC. To my amazement, somebody in the BBC music library replied and informed me that the tune was the opening of Igor Stravinsky's Symphony in Three Movements. I can still hear it in my head. Turbulent, chromatic. Jagged. Angry.

The only Stravinsky I had heard up to then was The Firebird, but this was something on a different plane altogether, so I vowed to make it my first brand new classical LP. On one of my Saturday trips to the west end, I had discovered the wonderland that was the Gramophone Exchange in Wardour Street, but never had enough money to buy a record. This time I managed somehow to save up enough for the LP. I remember the thrill of watching the vinyl disc sliding so easily into its beautiful shiny cover depicting a peacock against a plain white background. Over time the cover gradually yellowed and the sound quality deteriorated, but never has an LP been so treasured. Hard earned money well spent.

For a while I became a prefab-dwelling Stravinsky-head. Rite of Spring, Petrushka, Symphony in C, Symphony of Psalms, Les Noces. I still play his music whenever I get the chance. Dad thought it was all ear-splitting discordant noise, despite my attempts at converting him. Imagine my surprise when I discovered recordings of music by Stravinsky, Bartok and Poulenc among the cassettes he left behind when I cleared out my parents' council house decades later.

Money was always a problem, but my Saturday and holiday job income allowed me to buy more discs, not all classical music. I shared Charlie's enthusiasm for skiffle and folk music. I discovered jazz after hearing Miles Davis, Charlie Parker and Thelonious Monk. I love it still. Then, just before I left the prefab forever, it was the Beatles and the Rolling Stones. I discovered later that one of the Stones, drummer Charlie Watts, was brought up on a prefab estate not so far from ours.

Prefabulous Days

Chapter 20 | Moving on

1970

The BBC are as good as their word. Mandy, the PA, duly sends Harry and Olive a telegram to tell them when the Nationwide story will be transmitted. Olive then spreads the word at church and even sends an airmail letter to Charlie. He won't be able to see it in New Zealand of course. On the big day Olive, Harry, Tom, Bill and Agnes gather round the Dobson TV with beers and sandwiches. Twenty minutes in, they have been told, but that was only an approximation. Then, just as they are getting desperate, Bob Wellings shifts effortlessly from an item about the lack of Aylesbury ducks in Aylesbury, into a new studio link. Something like:

'Now, remember the prefabs built after World War Two? They were supposed to be temporary housing for ex-servicemen's families, scheduled to last for only ten years, but some were made of sterner stuff, and are still with us. Some of those prefab pioneer families, often looked down on as prefab scum, are keen to put the record straight once and forever. Two such families, now facing imminent demolition of their homes to make way for a shopping parade, are the Dobsons and Pattersons of the Friars Walk estate in London NW13. Jonathan Fairchild reports......'

After the show Olive says she's disappointed because there had been this other stuff about a batty old girl on another estate who had used her prefab as a sort of knick-knack museum. Jonathan hadn't mentioned that, had he? And she can't see what it has to do with the main story. Their story. Harry and Bill are both quite happy though, and don't think this matters – just the way these BBC people see things. Harry assumes their story will die pretty soon anyway, so what the hell, they've had their say and that's something.

Bill agrees. 'You know how it is with television, here today, gone tomorrow.'

Olive and Agnes both bask in the limelight for a day or two, and Bill gets his share of friendly ridicule at the pub. Tom's head mentions the item at the next staff meeting, without his permission.

But Harry was wrong. A few days later there's another letter on the mat, this time from a reporter on the Chiltern Echo. She asks if they would be interested in a feature article on what she calls the back story, leading to the demise of the prefab estate. Fair enough, he thinks, why not, but will Olive agree this time?

This time he treads carefully: 'Well dear it's up to you. But this should be a joint decision, with Bill and Agnes. All I'll say is that nothing bad has happened to us since the TV story broke. Of course the Echo is hardly in the same league, but they have covered the prefab saga from time to time in the past.'

Olive has changed her tune: 'Oh well, in for a penny I suppose. Only on condition I can have time to get my hair done. I don't want to be interviewed though. You and Bill have proved you are good at that, I have to admit.'

Harry calls in next door to ask Bill and Agnes if they want to join in, but Bill declines the offer this time: 'We're going over to Mary's place for a few days. Good luck anyway mate.'

Harry suspects Agnes isn't keen anyway. They also ask Tom if he's interested, and he agrees to come along for the ride if he's free.

This time the reporter is a plump middle-aged woman called Janet Wilkinson. After the usual tea and biscuits ritual she starts by explaining that her angle is not so much the imminent demolition of the remaining prefabs, but the failure of the campaign to prevent it. Olive makes it clear that she has nothing to say about that except it's gone on too long and has been very stressful for them both and their neighbours. Off the record please.

'Oh that's a shame Olive. Would it be OK to make that point without quoting you? Olive smiles and nods. She's clearly less than impressed by this overweight peroxide blonde, with as many bangles and cheap jewels as Madame Petulengro.

Janet dives into her briefcase and takes out a black box and a microphone and puts them on the dining table. She plugs the mike in and pushes two keys down together. One is labelled record, the other pause. She taps the mike and watches a tiny meter.

'OK to record this?'

Harry nods.

'They've dished us out with cassette recorders. The latest technology this. I've only used mine a couple of times. Supposed to make my life easier. Not sure why I learned shorthand. Here we go.'

Janet releases the pause key.

'So how long was your campaign Harry?'

'Depends on what you mean by campaign. It started in earnest three years ago, when someone on the tenants' association heard a rumour that the estate was to be knocked down to make way for a new housing and shopping development. Mind you, we've heard that before. Everyone knows the council's been trying to get rid of the prefabs for years. As you know all these prefabs built after the war were supposed to be temporary anyway. Ten years they reckoned. Me and Bill next door decided to organise a resistance campaign as soon as we got the first letter from the council two years ago.'

'Do you still have that letter?'

'Of course, we have kept all the correspondence. There's even a cutting from your paper.'

'Would you be prepared to let us see your files?'

'I don't see why not, none of it's confidential. Mind you, I will need to ask the other resistance fighters before I let you see them.'

'OK. So talk me through the campaign. How did you start?'

'Well, our first move was to get the opinions of as many neighbours as possible. If most people were going to be for the council's plans, then there would hardly be any point in resisting. Mind you their plans didn't include brand new flats at that stage. We simply knocked on every door and took notes. Usually of an evening when people were home from work or whatever. Out of a hundred and twelve prefab households, only a few people just shut the door in our faces, but most folk were at least interested enough to sign up for more information.'

'Was anyone for the idea right away?'

'Yes, a few. We listened to their views. They mostly wanted to know if the council would rehouse them in more modern houses. Fair enough.'

'Ok, what happened next?'

'Well, we took our findings to the tenants' association, and they tabled our report at their next meeting. You'll see the minutes in the file. Bill and I were at the meeting, and we both spoke in support of the report. To start with, they were non-committal, sitting on the fence as usual, and then they voted against a campaign, claiming they were concerned about possible social unrest. So we were on our own.'

'Why do you think they took that line? Do you think there was something else going on?'

'At the time we were just disappointed and puzzled, but later we were told by someone I can't name, that the association had been infiltrated by council sympathisers. Well, one family at least, who may have an ulterior motive.'

'Who's that then?'

'Nice try. You must be joking. This is on the record. All I am saying is that is what we were told by someone who thought we needed to know. On the QT of course.'

'A leak then.'

'If you like.'

'So how did your public meeting come about then?'

'Well, we were not happy about the refusal by the tenants' association to support a campaign. We knocked on doors again to tell everyone that we had hit a brick wall, and someone suggested a public meeting, so we went back to the council, and they said they would only agree to it if it was sanctioned by the tenants' association. As if by magic, the association changed their tune. I suppose they didn't want to be seen as siding with the council. As it turned out the meeting was a damp squib. Only a handful of tenants came along, and they didn't say much. The council people chose a time and place when most people would be at work or whatever. It was held at the town hall and they were very well prepared. It was a golden opportunity to launch their rehousing plan, not just to tenants but also to the press, including the Echo. I'm afraid we lost quite a few supporters that day.'

'So when did you give up the campaign?'

'Only a few weeks ago, when the council informed us that corrosion had been found in fabric of the prefabs. We've told them about that time and again, ever since we've lived here. I remember when a building inspector came round and had a look. The question is, why could the council not just maintain the prefabs properly in the first place, without having to rehouse everyone? Anyway, it was clear that we no longer had the support of most tenants, who found it hard to resist the bribe of new flats, with central heating and all that.'

'Thanks. I gather you were a bus conductor then Harry?

Harry nods.

'And you were involved in the bus strike in 1958?

'Yes, you have done your homework. I don't see what that has got to do with what we are supposed to be talking about though.'

'Well, we have been told that back then you were a shop steward in the TGU, and you held strike meetings here in this prefab. Is that true?'

'Yes – so what? Look, I am proud of what me and my brothers and sisters did in that dispute. If you really have done your homework, you'll know that we London bus workers were just trying to get a decent deal on pay and conditions for all public bus workers, all over the country. We had already got an acceptable deal for the London area, but we stayed out in support of the regional members. To do that we had to meet in our own time, off work premises. So what? That's all years ago.'

'Some people think your prefab demolition resistance campaign was a political stunt.'

'Who have you been talking to? Could it be the very same people who infiltrated the tenants' association? Someone who now stand to make a bob or two out of the development plan? Your turn to answer.'

'You know my answer, I can't reveal my sources. Maybe we should move on. How does your neighbour Bill Patterson fit into this?'

'I think you should ask him that, don't you? I will say that Bill has been a good friend to us since we met the day we both moved into our prefabs, and that our wives get on well too. And our kids. Our boys adored little Mary, and they are still friends. Bill's not a union man, and we often disagree about what's happening to our country, but in this case he agrees with me that the decision to knock the prefabs down should be in the hands of the people who have lived here for nearly twenty years, not in the grubby mitts of local councillors on the make.'

'You know we can't print unsupported allegations, Harry, so unless you have evidence of foul play, we can only put your suspicions to one side.'

'Of course, and you know I can't prove anything, but maybe you could have a poke around. For example. Did you know these prefabs are the only type made almost completely of aluminium, which is a relatively expensive metal? They're what's called a B2 or Airoh type, made by the Bristol Aeroplane Company, who had surplus stocks of aluminium after the war. Now, when buildings are demolished, the demolition contactors are responsible for disposing of the spoil. With brick houses this is just rubble, usually fit only for hard core, but in this case the company knocking down our homes will be able to sell the aluminium, at a premium. Do you know how much scrap aluminium fetches today?'

'No!'

'Me neither, but you are better placed than me to find out. Whatever it is, the contractor will get it, on top of their profits. Quite legal of course. Perhaps you could investigate who that is and how they got the contract.'

'Well, it's another angle I suppose…….. Ok to move on?

Harry nods again. He's in his stride now.

'Have you ever felt that other people look down on prefab dwellers?

'Good question. Where to start? As you know I was a bus conductor ever since the end of the war until I was promoted to Inspector. Bus conductors don't just sell tickets, they listen to what passengers say, and I can tell you from all those years that there was a lot of prejudice against prefab people, mostly at the beginning, when the estates were built. Over the years, people got used to them I suppose. I remember once, chatting to a charming lady on my bus, who told me that prefab estates were well known as Teddy Boy ghettos and state-created slums. At the time I was gobsmacked. I knew if I came out with what was in my head she would report me, so I kept quiet. She was a regular on that route, and very chatty, so I waited a week or two before I casually mentioned I lived on the Friars Walk estate. I never saw her on my bus again.'

'Why do you think people like her had that attitude?'

'Well, I'm not an educated man, but I think all prejudice is about fear, snobbery and ignorance. She was afraid of Teddy Boys because they had a bad press. She was obviously a gossip monger. I doubt she had ever been on a prefab estate and she wouldn't have known anyone who lived on one. Snobbery was once the domain of the rich, but after the first world war it became possible for middle class people to join the club. People like simple explanations, but life is complicated. She may have read a newspaper report that a teddy boy from a prefab estate had been sent to Borstal for criminal assault or some such. To her this meant all Teddy Boys must come from prefab estates and all prefab estates must be Teddy Boy breeding grounds. That's how prejudices are born. Fear, snobbery and ignorance.'

The interview is interrupted when Tom arrives. He has his own key. Janet stops the tape.

Harry greets his elder son: 'Hallo Tom. This is Janet, from the Echo.'

'Hi Janet, good of you to come out. What's this man been up to then?'

'Just been telling it like I see it son.'

'I'll bet.'

One drawback of aluminium prefabs Harry has not mentioned is their complete lack of sound insulation. Olive has been listening to every word from the front bedroom. At this point she emerges and offers to make another pot of tea.

Motion accepted *nem con.*

'That would be great Olive, but do you have any coffee?' Janet asks, as Olive edges round the utility style draw-leaf table to get to the kitchen.

Tom grins. Harry is inscrutable. Off-the-record chat is confined to small talk, mostly between Janet and Tom, who makes no bones about his ambition to get into journalism. Tea and coffee duly taken, Janet packs away her recorder, takes some photos of all three, and makes tracks for the newsroom before the rush hour gets going.

That evening, when the dining table has reverted to its proper function, Olive makes only one comment: 'I should have known she'd drink coffee……..'

Harry rolls his eyes, so Tom chips in. 'I think it's compulsory for journalists, Mum. By royal edict I expect. Something I'd have to get used if I ever get to be a journalist I suppose.'

Night falls over the sad remains of Friars Walk. Only two sets of windows light up.

Chapter 21 | Jobsworth

Transcript: Episode 11 of a series of podcasts recorded during the third Covid-19 lockdown, 2021. Written and read by Tom Dobson.

1956 - 1961

In earlier podcasts, I explained that I did casual work to fund things my parents could not afford, such as my school trip to France or buying a touring bike. My first job was at Woolworths, working as a Saturday boy and during school holidays. The job involved sweeping floors, bailing cartons and tending the boiler.

The best I can say for the Woolworths job is that it turned out to be an example of learning through negative experience. The manager was a diminutive humourless bully who hated his job and tried his best to make those under him hate theirs. His number-two, my immediate boss, a rather rakish Scottish chain-smoking queen-bee, had the difficult job of controlling the workforce, mostly nubile salesgirls penned up behind the old-fashioned counters on the shop floor. It was made clear from the start that I was not to have anything to do with them, presumably for fear of seduction of a minor. Fat chance.

Much of my time was spent operating a machine which compressed and bound cardboard boxes, not in itself very educational, but because this monster was housed adjacent to queen bee's cell, I couldn't help observing her behaviour, which seemed to consist of some kind of paperwork (maybe staff rotas or whatever,) being unpleasant to her girls, who were almost all better-looking than her, doing her make-up, smoking, drinking Nescafé, sucking up to the manager and haranguing me with her opinions on just about everything. I think she quite liked me, and did I like her, but things changed a bit when quite accidentally I caught her in the act of adjusting her suspenders. I think she assumed it was a deliberate act of voyeurism. I have to admit, she had surprisingly attractive legs.

Things went well enough until the run-up to Christmas, when I was called into the manager's office and was offered an opportunity to earn some overtime by transporting each day's takings to Woolworths' head office in Oxford Street. I was instructed to travel by train and tube to Oxford Circus, with a bulging black briefcase stuffed with a few thousand pounds worth of bank notes and bags of change. I was 15 years old and handcuffed to the briefcase. It did cross my mind that someone could hack my hand off and nick the takings, or maybe just murder me. I also contemplated absconding with the dosh and catching the next plane to Rio to lead a life of decadence and luxury. Neither happened; I now learn that this method of carrying money was regarded as normal.

Christmas over, out of the blue, the devil himself appeared one fine Saturday, broom in hand. He came disguised as a hearty lad called Bob, eager to please, employed to do exactly the same job as me. His unannounced addition to the staff was not explained, but I suppose I accepted it as just one of those things that employers do for no apparent reason. The only immediate disappointment was that I had to share the money usually found when sweeping the floor at the end of a trading day, which it was agreed should be treated as treasure trove, by tradition. I should have suspected his over-the-top bonhomie; it never occurred to me that he was a plant, really employed to spy on me and report back. I still have no idea why. Maybe it was the suspenders thing, or the flirting, or I just came across as a grammar school smart-arse. Or none of the above. Or all of the above.......

Anyway, sometime later I was dismissed on the grounds of stealing from my employer. The 'evidence' was a small collection of surplus goods, such as glass bottles of nail varnish, which had been sent down to the boiler room for incineration. When questioned I pointed out that chucking such things into a red-hot coke furnace was potentially dangerous, not least to the chucker. I also pointed out that the manager had previously allowed me to take home other surplus stock, for example some odd stick-on shoe soles, for personal use only. When I was sacked, one of my favourite shop girls told me who had engineered my downfall. Bob.

She also reckoned that Bob and the manager-from-hell were related in some way, therefore in cahoots. Bob had touched her up too. I like to imagine he eventually became the CEO of Woolworths UK, married suspender-lady and spawned a bunch of nasty offspring. Goodbye Woolworths, and good riddance. Vengeance was mine decades later when Woolworths went bust.

My next venture into retail was at Boots the chemist. For a while, my routine Saturday role was to assist an old retainer called Louis down in the basement. Tasks such as weighing out mothballs or washing soda, before bagging them up into blue paper bags. Pretty boring stuff, but Louis was a born raconteur, with a seemingly inexhaustible supply of World War One stories – a kind of proto-corporal Jones. The basis of his employment was evidently charity rather than necessity, and he was regarded with a mixture of kindness and mild irritation by some colleagues. I just listened to his war stories, true or not, and he was happy that I did.

The atmosphere at Boots was quite a change from the creepy nastiness of Woolworths. I don't remember having a boss – everyone seemed just to muck in, and there were lots of laughs. Some of the shop assistants, all female, used to come down to the basement for a sly fag on their breaks, and I got to know them a bit.

Pretty soon I was promoted to working on the shop floor, and when someone enquired about cameras or other photographic stuff I was called up. It was just assumed that, as a grammar school boy, I would be good at this, even though I actually knew next to nothing about the relative merits of various cameras and film stocks. I just read what it said on the packaging and bluffed my way from there on.

I had another occasional role, arising from being the only male counter assistant. Quite often men would come into the shop and pretend to be browsing. As soon as I was free, they would make a beeline, seeking condoms, or menstrual aids, often handing over surreptitious notes on scraps of paper. The sanitary towels ('STs') or tampons were no problem for me. Mary had told us boys all about them ages ago. I couldn't offer advice, so it was simply a matter of discreetly popping the packs into a brown paper bag, ringing the transaction up on the till and giving the change. Condoms were a problem though because Boots did not sell them, on principle, as a Catholic company in those days.

In retrospect I must have developed what are now called people skills, just by working at the counter – not just the business of serving customers but taking time to chat at less busy times and just being cheerful.

So far, these Saturday jobs were a means to specific ends before I took my O levels, but once I was in the sixth form, I felt the need to look for holiday jobs, partly to get out of the prefab and to contribute to the household budget, though my mum never asked for money. I found temporary jobs through the labour exchange. As a result, I bagged jobs at a gas depot, and two electronics factories.

The gas depot job came about as British Oxygen had decided to update its customer records from masses of documents in rows of filing cabinets, to a card index system. This meant endless hours of transferring customer details to the cards by hand. I think my title was something like clerical assistant. The bloke I assisted was not much older than me. The main reason he needed assistance was that he spent much of his time ogling girls in the typing pool, clearly visible in an adjacent office, and pinging them with paper clips projected by means of elastic bands. What did I learn? Not much, except annoying girls is dumb way to seduce them.

The next job was rather more interesting and formative. The labour exchange pointed me toward a short-term post as an assistant progress chaser in a subsidiary of GEC, the biggest electrical and electronic manufacturer in the UK. It took only a day or two to work out that the progress chaser, let's call him Bill, was no good at chasing progress, but for whatever reason had not been sacked. At least he wasn't chasing women. As far as I could see anyway.

The company had a contract to make seven gigantic and very complex X-Ray machines for Saudi Arabia, but they were way behind schedule because every time any one of the thousands of component parts which made up the machines went missing, the entire production line simply stopped, and the workers played cards or whatever until they turned up. Or not.

Nothing much happened until Bill told me to look into some missing components. Nuts, bolts, resistors, whatever. The supplier was adamant that the components had been delivered weeks ago and quoted the delivery note details. I went over to stores and found them easily enough. They had been put in the wrong place. There didn't seem to be any official way to get them to where they were needed, so I just signed them out and took them down to the production line myself.

Shop floor eyebrows went up, meaningful looks were exchanged, intakes of breath were heard. It turned out that what I had done was highly irregular, and it was quietly made clear that it was not in my interests to do this kind of thing in future. Then I got it – the longer it took to complete the contract, the better the chances of the shop floor workers keeping their jobs and having an easy time. The word 'union' was not uttered in my presence, but I overheard it muttered a few times in my travels around the factory.

Sadly, my best efforts were in vain. The deadline was missed, the Saudis pulled out. The company was left with seven incomplete X-Ray machines and my contract period expired.

However, before I left, I was called in to see the personnel officer, where I was told that Bill's progress chasing days were over and his job was mine if I wanted it. No need to decide straight away – just think about it. He knew I was heading for university when I left school, so he was really nice about it when I turned down the offer. I wonder to this day whether I made a mistake.

The last job was with Goodman's, a company who made some of the best loudspeakers in the world during the sixties hi-fi boom. Though my job was in the machine shop, operating a heavy-duty metalworking lathe to make loudspeaker magnets covers, this place fascinated me, as someone who had built his own audio amplifier and turntable. Apart from the money, I stayed there mainly for lunchtimes, when I would explore other parts of the factory and chat to other workers. I relished a hard day's work, deafened by the machine-shop din, and became intoxicated by the unique smell of hot metal and lathe scurf. Above all I loved the works canteen. I now see my preference for canteen dining as a thread that has run through most of my working life. I miss it now. Victoria Wood nailed it all right.

Though the need for employment arose mainly because I needed money to buy things which my parents could not have afforded or to contribute to the family budget, I now see there was an unforeseen bonus – these jobs were learning experiences which I now value as highly as any amount of official education.

Chapter 22 | Harry has an idea

1970 / 1982

The Echo article is published a week later. Harry and Bill have already become local heroes following the Nationwide TV news item, much to their wives' satisfaction. Well, if not heroes, at least recognisable in town. This newspaper article is the icing on their cake. The reporter, Janet Wilkinson, has been as good as her word, sticking to the history of the resistance campaign, and leaving out most of Harry's more contentious, if not exactly libellous, comments. She has included a typically anodyne comment from the council, simply pointing out that most estate residents have moved out and many have accepted new accommodation in the borough.

Harry has been thinking about what their life will be like in a new flat. He and Olive have talked about little else. Now it's a reality, they are both apprehensive, even though the council is bending over backwards to make the transition as easy as possible for them. Council staff will pack up their worldly goods and install them in the flat, free of charge, sort out the post office notification, facilitate electricity supply transfer and connect the gas. They can get a phone installed if they wish. Yes please says Olive.

Janet has written a nice thank-you letter and promised to stay in touch. She has had a word with her editor about a possible follow-up piece once they have moved – perhaps focusing on the wives this time.

Harry, always the worrier, has had a bad dream about the demolition – bulldozers crushing the prefab while they are having their dinner. But he and Bill know already that the prefabs are not simply knocked down, but carefully disassembled. Throughout the demolition process, they have made a habit of chatting up the site manager, Declan, a genial Irishman who seems quite sympathetic to their cause. At first he had been understandably cagey, but lately he had been quite informative about their contract and their relationship with the council. Strictly off the record of course. He was the source of Harry's unpublished comment about the profit the contractor might make on selling the aluminium for scrap. Decent fellow, Declan.

He has also told Harry that his company do not pull all the prefabs apart for scrap, because there is a market in selling them for re-assembly and re-use. This is a revelation. It seems that Airoh prefabs in particular are in demand by companies and public institutions for use as temporary office or storage purposes. He and Bill should have worked this out when they watched some of their neighbours' homes taken lifted by crane and taken away whole on giant articulated lorries. For example, Declan says, two of them are being fitted out for a well-known engineering plant in the West Midlands. Much depends on the state of each prefab though, so only the well-kept units are likely to end their days in some other company's back yard.

Harry is fascinated by all this and goes off to do some research at the public library, where he is well known as a self-teaching regular. This information has sparked a train of thought in his fertile brain. Does it always have to be about profit? Why should the two remaining prefabs not be donated for posterity, reminders of the past? Would this not be good for the council's rather tattered reputation? One snag though, Harry's name is mud at the council. Worse than mud. The more the thinks about the idea, the more determined he becomes, so he asks Olive what she thinks. For once she's all for it, so the next move is to consult the other members of the gang of four.

Agnes is enthusiastic. 'I love it Harry – why should everything be about money? I would love our grandchildren to be able to see how we lived. A prefab in a museum would be so much more appealing to kids than reading about it or looking at photos. I can imagine them on a school visit being fascinated by the kitchen and bathroom especially. Go for it!'

Bill, typically, is wary. 'Aye, it's a good idea, but I can't see the contractor buying it, let alone the council. They have contractual obligations. And who's going to persuade them? We're not exactly in their good books, are we? They must have a pretty big file on you by now Harry. Marked in red I should think.'

'Well you never get anywhere unless you try, and it could be a way to make it up with the council after all these years. I've heard the new leader of the council, this Mrs Hancock, is a reformer, with a track record of getting things done.

But you're right Bill, it would be better coming from someone else. None of us is getting any younger, and we've enough on our plates with all this disruption. But if we don't get on with it, our prefabs will just disappear.'

Olive has an idea too. 'Perhaps Tom might be interested? He still lives in the area and it wouldn't hurt his career to pull something like this off, would it? He would know who to talk to and all that. He's keen on anything to do with education.'

'Hands up for calling Tom then!'

Four hands go up.

'So who's got some coins for the phone?

Fired with enthusiasm, Harry trudges through the rain to the one-and-only public phone box which has served the estate since 1949. For once the coin drops and he's through to Tom second go. Tom, who has been a bit down lately, is glad of an excuse to come over: 'On the face of it dad, I think this is a brainwave. Count me in, but don't do anything rash. I can come over tomorrow evening if you like.'

'OK, come for supper. Can you stand more fish and chips? You could stop at the chippy on the way over. No, I won't do anything rash, but I'll keep my thinking cap on. You know me.'

'I do dad, I do. See you about six tomorrow. Warm up the plates.'

Tom prefers his fish and chips on a warm plate. Something he picked up at University, strangely. His mum approves.

As promised, he breezes in the following evening. He seems quite elated. Drowning his chips with vinegar, Harry comes out with something unexpected.

'Remember when the TV people were here, were you serious when you said something about becoming a journalist?'

'Oh, I forgot to tell you. I told you I worked on the student newspaper at university. I really enjoyed that, and one of my tutors encouraged me to submit some of my work to the local paper there. They liked my stuff and wanted me to do more, but I was put off by my head of department, Prof. Simmons, who thought I was spending too much time on it, at the expense of my studies, so I only wrote one or two more articles. Well, as you know I do like my job as a schoolteacher, but I have been thinking about doing some more journalism on the side. Trouble is the day job is so demanding just now, so that idea is on the back burner for now. Why do you ask?'

'Just a loose end really. You always did bite off more than you can chew, and I was afraid you were off chasing a new rainbow again.'

'Mmm. You could be right. Don't worry about it. I know you think I don't stick at things enough, but let's say university has changed me for the better. I admit I was fascinated by the way the TV crew did their job, and it stirred up my journalism ambitions a bit. I reckon I could do a better job than that toffee-nosed reporter guy if I could get into radio or TV. The newspaper article too, though that reporter was obviously better at her job, I thought. Anyway, I do have some thoughts about your idea.'

'OK, what do you reckon?'

'Well, I think you are right about keeping your distance. And the council might realise I'm your son, so that might put them off too. I think we should make a proposal to Marshalls and let them deal with the council if they bite. In fact, the council doesn't need to be involved at all if the demolition agreement gives the contractor the exclusive right to own the demolished properties and do whatever they like with them, which is the usual arrangement. If Marshalls want to inform the council, that's their business. Maybe the first move should be to have another word with your friend Declan, to find out who runs the business. They are pretty well-known company, and like all contractors they will want to stay in their clients' good books, so I bet they would talk to the council anyway at some stage. They can make the point about the idea making the council look good.

Come to think of it, this might be an opportunity for me to get back to some journalism. If I get on with making the idea work, I can document the project and write it up as a feature, assuming nobody else has already done something similar. What do you think?'

Harry is smiling in that way he has. 'Well, I'm certainly willing to talk to Declan and let you know what he says. Just as you suggest, as a first move. Then I can hand the whole thing over to you if that's OK. Would you like to involve Janet at the Echo? She did offer to stay in touch, and she might be able to help.'

'Maybe, but not yet. If we got as far as getting an agreement with Marshalls, then we could maybe let her know, but for now, let's keep it under our hat. And that should include Bill and Agnes too.'

'Ok. What kind of museum do you think might be interested?'

'Well, not a local museum. I think it should be national. After all, the whole post-war prefab thing is already a slice of social history. It's a prime example of progress through ingenuity and science. After all, Churchill is supposed to have come up with it. If I'm right, then it should be one of the national museums in London or some other major city. Aim high, I say. I'll make a start of writing up a proposal. After I finished my marking, of course. I'll write to Charlie as well – he should have a say too. It's where he grew up as well. You can let Bill and Agnes know. Mary too.'

A few weeks later, before the prefabs are demolished, a young woman knocks at the Dobsons' door. She is perhaps in her early twenties. She carries a brown leather briefcase. If Harry or Olive had been in, they might have thought she was from the council, or perhaps a museum. Failing to get any response, she goes next door, to the Patterson's and rings their doorbell. Electric, of course. Agnes answers the door, and the visitor explains she is an undergraduate who has been following the Friarscroft Way stories on TV and in the papers. She seems genuine enough, so Agnes invites her in, and she explains that she is researching prefab estates for her sociology degree thesis. Agnes is not sure what to do, so she suggests that Miss Smith returns when the Dobsons are in. She agrees to pass the message on. The student gives Agnes her contact details.

With only days left before the move, Agnes thinks it over. She's not keen about Bill meeting such an attractive young woman. She's had enough of that kind of trouble over the years. Miss Smith? The student story could be fake. She might be just another journalist or a spy of some kind. Whatever, Agnes keeps the matter to herself and it goes no further.

Twelve years later Tom finds himself supervising a secondary school trip to the London Museums. The last stop is the Science Museum in South Kensington. Running out of time, he takes them through the floors he thinks will interest his charges most, but two of the kids have spotted a special exhibition in the basement, all about England in the fifties. He takes them downstairs, leaving the others to eat buns and drink pop, supervised by his colleague Irene. The exhibition has been well worth the entrance fee, but Tom is anxious not to miss their train home.

Suddenly he finds himself back at No. 35 Friars Walk. Not a fantasy or a time warp, but for real. The museum people have abandoned the outer shell, and reconstructed the inside, so you just wander into the interior, willy-nilly. There it all is, the kitchen, complete with counter, cupboards, fridge and a pine table, bathroom, front room, and two bedrooms, all arranged according to the standard floor plan.

The two girls think their teacher is freaking out, gibbering on about how this is probably the prefab he grew up in. If not, the one next door. On the train home, he babbles on about the prefabs, how they were made in a factory, the estate and some of his memories, but his audience soon tires. The next day he phones the museum to confirm whether the display is indeed from Friars Walk, but they are unable to help much. Their records don't show quite how they came by the prefab interior. Later, some member of museum staff remembers that two Airoh prefabs turned up out of the blue a few years ago and they have been used for archive storage at one of their depots outside London. The current display was reconstructed using bits of both of them.

Harry asks what will happen when the exhibition finishes. It's due to be closed in a months' time. The prefab interior might go to a regional museum, or it will most likely be destroyed. Tom organises a mystery tour for the Dobsons and the Pattersons. They know they are going to London, but that's all. Inside the reconstructed prefab interior, Harry and Bill are lost for words, silenced for the only time in living memory. Olive and Agnes weep.

In the museum canteen, Olive is the first to speak. 'What a shock. Shame Charlie and Mary can't be here to see this.' They never do.

Chapter 23 | Fugue

Transcript: Episode 12 of a series of podcasts recorded during the third Covid-19 lockdown, 2021. Written and read by Tom Dobson.

1961

Imagine me, a small skinny young man pulling a suitcase strapped to a converted folding shopping trolley, scanning the departure board for the next train to Newhaven harbour, bound for Lyon, via Dieppe and Paris. My parents and friends thought I must be mad. It even scares me now, just thinking about it.

My idea was to fill some of the time gap left after an exam resit and taking up the offer I had from a redbrick university of a place to study English and French literature. I had already come up with the idea of simply heading to France on my own, albeit with minimal resources. Today's equivalent would be a back-packing gap year, which is now commonplace, but back then it would have been regarded as quite adventurous, not say completely foolhardy, especially for a prefab boy with little or no means of support. Like back packs, gap years had not yet been invented.

What I did have was a return train ticket to Lyon, and the promise of a job as a *moniteur* (group leader) in a *colonie de vacances* (summer camp) in Savoie, thanks to a rather quaint organisation in London specialising in international educational work placements. A condition of taking this job was to attend a '*stage*' – a training course, to be held in the countryside near Lyon. Naturally this was to be conducted in French. In the event, I decided not to wait for the training course, so one fine day I set off to travel by train and ferry to Lyon and take my chances.

In the sixties Lyon was hardly a tourist destination and I could not have afforded a hotel anyway, but I had taken the precaution of keeping my old YHA membership up. I found a Youth Hostel a few kilometres north of the city, right by the river Saône. In principle I was limited to a three day stay, but as things turned out I stayed there for a month, having done a nifty deal with the genial warden Lucien, an old-style French hippy, who allowed me to stay for free as long as I did some routine work for him from time to time – cleaning mostly.

I have tried to locate this hostel, one of those lovely old neglected mini chateaux you find all over France, gently decaying in the sunshine, but it seems to have vanished, at least according to Google Maps. I loved my stay here, passing my time walking the hills, taking the odd bus trip into town, browsing the central market in Lyon and chatting to those passing through the youth hostel, but after a couple of weeks my meagre savings were exhausted. Then something happened which not only solved that problem but changed my rather limited view of humanity for the better.

A young couple turned up, having travelled from England on foot and by bus. They both had foreign accents and seemed to be very much in love. She was a tiny blonde, and he was a skinny fellow who just radiated energy and joie de vivre. We hit it off immediately. I learned that he was Polish, she was German, they were married, and they lived in Ladbroke Grove. He had survived the Nazi camps, settled in post-war London as a young man and married a German student there. He had also changed his name to Leslie and now worked as a delivery van driver.

He could remember life in the concentration camps but was not keen to talk about it. He did not know what happened to his parents. I was astounded that he had married a German girl, and we did talk about that. His view was that the only point in remembering the past is to learn. For him the present and future were what mattered. He also told me with pride that as a boy he had been champion boxer, with a physique to match. He claimed that he survived by entertaining the camp guards in the boxing ring. When I got to know both of them better, we talked about how their relationship flourished despite attitudes in post-war London, where racism and xenophobia were the norm.

My lack of funds became an acute problem, and it turned out that my new friends were also in need of some money. Leslie came up with an elegant solution. The most regular overnight hostellers were long distance cyclists (usually German!) who would typically arrive late in the evening, exhausted, stagger into bed and disappear at sparrow-fart next morning. Leslie had noticed that they usually left behind empty soft drink bottles, and he had found out that they were returnable at any shop selling such thirst quenchers. The nearest shop was in a village a few kilometres away on the far side of the river. Each empty bottle attracted a few francs on return.

So a plan was hatched, and we collected these bottles for a day or two, then headed over the bridge to redeem them, toiling uphill in the heat of the afternoon to the tiny village on the west bank of the Saône. I think it was called Saint-Cyr-au-Mont D'or. The plan worked, but only after much protest and shouting by the shop owner, who tried to avoid forking out. She was so scary that on my own I would probably have abandoned the enterprise, but not so our Polish leader. For him this was just a skirmish, to be enjoyed rather than feared. Eventually she gave in when threatened with les flics, (the cops). We repeated this exercise several times later, despite her ever-sullener hostility. It was just enough to last us until

Leslie and his wife moved on and I got the phone call summoning me to my summer camp training course.

This was duly held at a training centre up in the foothills of the Alps, a few kilometres west of Lyon. Lots of hearty physical exercise and child psychology theory, all conducted in French of course. Fortunately the food was excellent. I passed with flying colours, despite the ice-cold hosing down sessions after long walks and dire warnings about the dangers of sunstroke. I learned more French in that fortnight than at any time later.

On the day the Colonie was due to start, a convoy of buses rolled up, full of the sons and daughters of Lyon municipal bus company employees, their parents and the staff who were to run the show, organised by the bus drivers' trade union. I clambered aboard the first bus, still lugging the world's first wheelie suitcase. This brave caravan then ground its way East, up the lower alpine slopes to a remote château in Savoie, which was to be our communal home for the next twelve long weeks.

On arrival, my new colleagues, who evidently knew the ropes, organised the kids into age groups, and the buses disappeared with weeping mothers and bored fathers. I was summoned to the admin office, and given a pep talk by the *directeur* and his sidekick. I was then taken to my allocated quarters, a dank room at the base of a medieval tower, with orders to report for duty the next morning.

I soon gathered that the grim director and his sinister henchman were moonlighting schoolteachers – a common practice apparently. After some preliminary haranguing masquerading as a staff meeting, Monsieur le Directeur was conspicuous by his absence as his number two bullied anyone he could, whether staff or children. I learned a few years later that this too was common practice in French secondary schools. The real work was done day and night by my fellow moniteurs, mostly students, and the support staff. This genial workforce routinely ignored the gang of two and just did what they were good at – inspiring and cherishing disadvantaged but streetwise city kids.

Monsieur le Directeur must have been remarkably stupid, or perhaps devious, as he put me in charge of the youngest children – four or five-year olds – who naturally found my French a bit hard to understand. A moment's thought ought to have revealed that this age group had to be the most difficult to care for. Nevertheless, I got on well with my colleagues, and I enjoyed the copious after-hours drinking sessions and the terrific food kept back and cooked by our lovely Spanish cook. I still occasionally cook a great Moroccan chicken casserole from a recipe I learned from that wonderful lady after hours.

The children all came from a vast working-class high-rise estate on the outskirts of Lyon, where survival of the fittest was the name of the game. The appeal of regular country walks and craft sessions was bound to be somewhat limited. The boys wanted adventure, so the first reaction of my lot to nature was to destroy the environment in war games. Craft sessions for the older boys were similarly oriented toward one or other form of weaponry, while the girls mostly pined for their mothers or deliberately wet their pants to dodge activities they didn't like.

Both boys and girls universally hated the afternoon siesta, which appeared to be compulsory, probably victims of a Napoleonic decree or some such. It wasn't much fun for us either as the kids were diabolically adept at staying awake and causing trouble.

The *Colonie de Vacance* network operated within an ideology based on the healthy-body-healthy-mind concept, rather like the Scout movement or the American summer camps. I have often wondered why the idea never really caught on in Britain, as a well-intentioned post-war attempt to bring happiness to working-class children and to widen their experience beyond their home circumstances. Sadly the colonie movement has been replaced by profit-making networks – a convenience for well-off parents who want to dump their kids during the school holidays.

When the buses returned twelve weeks later to take the kids back home, my friend Roland invited me to quit with him and travel by scooter down to the Côte-d'Azur to catch up with a girl he had fallen for. So off we went, Roland and I, riding due south down the incredible *Route Napoléon* as far as Digne, where we pitched his faded orange tent. I had a few weeks before my university deadline, and the Mediterranean beckoned.

Roland was unsuccessful in his quest. I think he did manage to get an invite to the home of the girl he was after, whose father was wealthy and influential, but I suspect he was playing out of his league. I still had time to kill, but the money was running out again, so we somehow got a part-time job with an Italian family, *selling cacaoettes* (chocolate-coated peanuts) to Scandinavian and German tourists on the beach at Juan-les-pins. (I like to think we were really working for the Mafia.) This was easy money, exploiting the rich, dependent on the time-honoured skills of spoilt children to extract goodies from their parents. We commuted daily from our tent in Digne, and ate frugally, beachcombers in one of the most popular hangouts of the global rich.

I was briefly tempted by an offer to join a monastery on a nearby island – no strings, not even a belief in God – but finally I decided to return England and the prospect of the drizzle and fog of the East Midlands. My inner jury is still out on whether I made the right choice.

The journey back was horrendous, and I was anxious about finally leaving home. When I turned up at the prefab, mum didn't recognise me. She thought the tan was fake, and I found it strange to speak English. She thought I was showing off again.

A van turned up to take my trunk away, and I took the train from St. Pancras to be a full time undergraduate. The next time I returned to Friars Walk, Mum had rented out the back bedroom where Charlie and I had grown up, strictly against the rules. For a while, the prefab would crop up in my dreams, and I would feel a sense of security and peace.

Chapter 24 | Charlie remembers

2020 and 1947 - 2021

Email message (05/04/20)

charliedobbo@gmail.com to tomdobson@hotmail.co.uk

Hi bro. Thanks for your last. I have had a good go at your blog and I must say my first reaction was why are you and this Frances doing this? I don't really get this kind of stuff, memoirs and all that. I know you got talked into it, but I think it's an obsession with you now, especially the prefab stuff. Some of the other memoirs are pretty interesting – loads of stuff I didn't know about in fact. You do have the knack – I liked quite a lot of your accounts of teaching and journalism. Far more readable than our life on the estate. Anyway, now you want my memories. I'm not keen, but I don't want to disappoint you, so I'll do my best. Actually, Maia seems very keen on this – she's always been fascinated by our family. So different from hers I suppose. I don't mind being named. I think all this false name stuff is just cowardly. But for God's sake don't let anyone have my contact details.

Email message (07/04/20)

tomdobson@hotmail.co.uk to charliedobbo@gmail.com

Well I suppose I asked for that. Why are we doing this? Frances has a special interest in Friars Walk – that's all I can say for now. Did you read all the comments on the prefab blog posts? I must admit this has become something of a Frankenstein's monster, and I admit to being obsessed. I just love writing, and I am really interested in the anti-prefab angle. The thing is, all these people we grew up with seem to remember you rather than me, and I'm not surprised. When I was pedalling away on the fretwork machine, or on the bike, or building radio sets, you were out there on the street, chasing one or other girl, fighting with the bad boys, or learning the three-chord trick on the guitar I made for you. You were Mr popular, and I was always proud of you for that. You even managed to make dad laugh, for which you deserve a medal. In any case, this is for France's research, not my blog. She's just trying to write the story of the post-war prefab boom, partly through the memories of the likes of us. Of course we won't divulge your contact details – I never do. Please thank Maia for bullying you into this. She's a treasure.

Email message (23/06/20)

charliedobbo@gmail.com to tomdobson@hotmail.co.uk

So sorry this has taken so long. Frances – are you more than friends? At your age, Dear me. My turn to confess this time – I have really enjoyed doing this. It's also made me think more about my life, so different from yours. Leaving school at 15, joining the merchant navy, girl in every port (I wish!), playing in the band, meeting Maia, deciding to stay in NZ, hitting the Auckland music scene, working in the wine trade, settling in Titirangi, two kids of our own – the whole nine yards. It's a very strange thing to sit on the beach and think back to our prefab days. And I'm really sorry I was so shitty about your blog. The more I read it, the more I understand what motivates you, but I still find much of it boring. What I most remember is how I looked up to you when we were kids, even though we fought so much, as brothers do I guess. I was embarrassed by your bloody plywood pipe racks and wooden toys, but I can now reveal that I was secretly proud of you. Not to mention the home-built wireless and hi-fi. Looking back, the difference between us is that you made the best of the hand we were dealt, and you're still doing that. I just ran away at the first chance I got, then built a new life. We were both right, but in different ways. Nobody can change the past, but there's no harm in thinking about it I guess, so long as it's not just an escape from the present. Prefab memoirs attached!

Attachment: Charlie's memories

I can't remember moving into the prefab, and I don't remember what my brother Tom calls the old house at all. I suppose to begin with, Tom used to protect me, and I did look up to him. But I suppose later on he used to annoy me, and we used to fight over anything at all, according to mum. Tom reckons our dad banned us from playing in the street, but I didn't know that. My earliest memories are mum playing the mandolin and us listening to children's hour on the wireless. I suppose dad must have abandoned the ban at some point because the things I remember best either happened in the street or up on the hill behind the estate, or at school.

All those years back the estate roads were quiet. Not many vehicles used the estate road and drivers usually drove slowly as they knew us kids would be out and about playing in the road. We were rather good at dodging them anyway. One of my favourite games was roller skate hockey, mimicking the Wembley Lions ice hockey team that I'd seen at the Empire Pool, thanks to an obliging family up the road. During the real matches ice hockey sticks would often get broken and if so we'd rush to the front of the ice rink and ask for the broken sticks, which we took home and repaired with angle brackets and insulation tape. The puck was a round taped up tobacco tin. The only disadvantage was there was no area of the estate road that was flat, so one team always had a disadvantage of having to skate uphill.

I remember a big day in 1953 (but not as big and grand as the Queen's Coronation) on the estate, with flags and banners and people clapping and cheering as one of the tenants returned home from fighting in the Korean War.

In our back garden our dad built a brick coal bunker and every summer he ordered a ton (20 bags) of coal as you'd get a special summer discounted rate. When it was delivered my job was to count the bags as some of the coal men were not always honest. Each bag had to be carried on the coal man's back from the road to our prefab which was probably 50 yards or so. When they had finished mum always made them a cup of tea. In those days we didn't use mugs only cups and saucers, the coal men would then tip the hot tea from the cup into the saucer to cool it and then slurp it from the saucer.

Milk was delivered six days a week by the United Dairy. First by horse and cart then by electric milk float. I remember one Christmas 'Jim the milkman' had been given a tot at so many prefabs that he was well and truly sozzled. He wasn't in any fit state to drive the horse and cart back to the depot, so someone took the horse and cart to the top of the estate and then the horse took over the journey back. The horse had done the journey twice a day six days a week for so many years it knew the way.

'Jim the milkman' was a likeable chap always ready to help anyone. When someone's rabbit contracted Myxomatosis, they couldn't face doing the kindest thing in that situation themselves, so they left a note in their empty milk bottle asking Jim to put it out of its misery, he did just that with no fuss. He was always helping folks out. I remember as a kid saving the newly mown grass cuttings and feeding it to the horse. Eventually the horse and cart was replaced by an electric milk float, it was never the same.

There was a sequel. Something that happened right outside our side door. One day we heard the whine of the float as it went by, then a loud bang, then a lot of swearing and a child wailing. The swearing came from the milkman, the wailing came from a toddler whose toy pushchair was firmly wedged under the milk float. It took some getting out, and when it finally emerged the pushchair was a mangled wreck, but its passenger, a teddy bear, only had mild concussion and some loss of stuffing, easily mended by a kind teddy bear nurse. Bread was delivered by the Co-Op bakery. The rag and bone man came around the estate on a regular basis crying out loudly. 'Any old iron rag bone' if you gave him a decent bundle of clothes he'd give you a goldfish in a plastic bag full of water, us kids thought that was great.

I used to play with a gang of boys in those days, even though our parents disapproved. We used to think up all kinds of tricks to play on other kids, especially girls. We also targeted kids from the posh houses who used to pass by the estate. One little girl used to ride her Gresham Flyer on the main road just outside the estate. We distracted her and put a banger in the little boot of her tricycle, and it blew the lid off. I think her mother reported the incident to the residents association. She called us prefab hooligans.

One of my first girlfriends told me a weird story. Whilst going out of the estate on a lovely summers day she passed one of the prefabs back garden and saw the bloke that lived there sitting in a deckchair sunbathing, dressed only in a swimming costume. She thought nothing of it, but on her return home much later that evening he was still there. She thought it was strange, as the temperature had dropped considerably by then, but the following day she discovered that when his family had arrived back home they found he was in fact stone dead!

Miss Timpson was the head mistress when I started in the infants, Mr Potter was the headmaster of the juniors. I was caned by him for being in a gang, not that we did anything wrong just that we called ourselves the Marmite gang! Mr Denton, the deputy head took us for PE in the hall upstairs. I remember the two gigantic hymn books hanging up in the hall for the children to sing from. Also in the hall were the shields of the four school 'houses' Nelson (blue) Faraday (yellow) Elgar (red) Goldsmith (green). Going back to Mr Denton, I was sent to him for messing about in Miss Lamb's art class. She said, 'Tell Mr Denton what you've done'. He was teaching Class 1 at the time, in one of the HORSA huts. I knocked on his door. When he called me in I told him what I'd done, he took me into the cloakroom between the two classrooms of the HORSA buildings and gave me three lashes of the cane on my backside. He always had a row of lads waiting outside his class to give them the cane. I got the cane for leaving the jar of water on the desk after an art lesson! There was a boy called Leonard who received the cane 36 times in one term! I never messed about in art again! Mr Denton smoked cigarettes and I always remember him on playground duty with a cup of tea slurping it through his teeth.

(HORSA is the acronym for the 'Hutting Operation for the Raising of the School-Leaving Age', a programme of hut-building in schools introduced by the UK Government to support the expansion of education under the Education Act 1944 to raise the compulsory education age by a year to age 15.)

I remember that one day I got fed up and went home soon after lunch. Mum got stroppy and walked me to school next day, warning the teacher she should see that I stayed there. She did. I hated lessons but I have since learned that there are times in this life when you have to wear stuff you'd rather do without.

But things changed when we had to sit the 11+ exam. I failed it because I hadn't paid attention much in class. Unlike my brother Tom, who was in the year above me. He was a typical swot, but I just loved being outside playing or doing sport, specially football and cricket. Some kids supported Spurs, others were keen on Arsenal or Chelsea, and there were a lot of fights about who was the best. We all used to collect cigarette cards specially the football heroes like Stanley Matthews and Danny Blanchflower.

I don't remember that much about Miller's Way secondary modern, except flirting with girls, playing for the school first eleven and joining a skiffle band called the Merry Millers. We were inspired by Lonnie Donnegan. I started on the tea chest base, but I wanted to play the guitar and I didn't have one, so my brother Tom who was a dab hand at fretwork made me one in his woodwork classes at his grammar school. Somebody taught me the 3-chord trick and I was away. Cumberland Gap, Dead or Alive, Putting on the Style.

By then I had learned how to keep out of trouble. The teachers were mostly useless and nobody learned much. I didn't fancy woodwork or metalwork, but I did like art. The girls used to do typing and domestic science, which was mostly cooking. One of my best girlfriends was called Chiara, and she used to give me food she cooked, and just to be with her I asked if I could swop woodwork for domestic science. This was unheard of, but they let me do it. For all their faults, the teachers were quite progressive for the times I guess. Me and Chiara used to cook Italian dishes we cooked from recipes someone's mum lent us. Chiara was from Italy. My parents hated the spaghetti and tagliatelle I brought home, but we had some laughs when dad couldn't manage to get them into his mouth without getting sauce all down his shirt, and he never pronounced her name properly. Chiara could swear in Italian and she was beautiful. She didn't live on the estate, and when she came home with me, there were some funny looks. Looking back I think she got a fair bit of racist crap, probably because of the war I guess, but she had been well trained by her brilliant mum Mirabella, so she was excellent in the use of bad language and rude gestures. Chiara was the best thing in my teenage life, and we did really love each other. Sometimes she used to sing in the band, and years later I heard she became an actress and ballad singer in America.

Tom's first guitar fell to bits quite quickly, so he made another one for me, and by the time I left school I could play loads of chords and even some lead-guitar riffs, and I joined another band. We used to do gigs at weddings and parties, and even earned a few bob. But it was just a hobby, and my mum and dad were badgering me about what to do after school. The so-called careers teacher was useless, so I went with Tom to our local library, where they had lots of careers stuff, and I looked up information about becoming a chef, but that meant going to college. I wanted something that didn't involve sitting in any more classrooms, but the message came through loud and clear that you couldn't walk out of school with no O levels and expect to saunter straight into a brilliant career and make loads of money.

I thought about the police and the military, but for some reason I always fancied the navy because two of our cousins did that, so I joined the local sea cadets for a while. This was a new world for me. We were a long way from the sea, but we did get to row a large boat on the reservoir a few times, which was fun, and the old salts who ran the sessions were great old blokes with all kinds of far-fetched memories of their lives at sea. One of them, Danny, had been a ship's cook in the merchant navy for many years, and he had some brilliant stories to tell. He explained that if I was serious I would have to start at the bottom rung and apply to go to a training school, and he would give me a reference. He also told me a lot about his life, good and bad. Looking back, he was right about most of it. So I was the first to move out of the prefab, bound for Plymouth. I was dead lucky – these days you need a degree or something to become a ship's cook, and there are few Brits in the game now.

A few years after our prefab had been pulled down I had sailed the world in and out of the kitchens of the Shaw Savill liners Southern Cross and Northern Star, feeding officers and passengers bound for South Africa, Australia and New Zealand. My favourite was New Zealand, and eventually I built a new life here. One day, sitting on our veranda, I watched a bungalow being towed along the Northern Wairoa river on a raft, near Dargaville. It reminded me of my prefab days somehow.

Chapter 25 | Mary, the girl next door

2020

Email message (16/05/20)

charliedobbo@gmail.com to tomdobson@hotmail.co.uk

Hi bro. I'm glad you liked my memories stuff. Quite disjointed obviously, but I just wrote it as I remembered things. As we agreed, I have left out any personal stuff to do with our parents or next door, so I was surprised when you asked about Mary. I see what you mean though. She was our sister really. It's ages since I heard from her, so I guess it would be OK to ask how she would feel about writing something. I wouldn't hold my breath though.

Email message (17/05/20)

tomdobson@hotmail.co.uk to charliedobbo@gmail.com

Thanks Charlie.

Email message (27/07/20)

charliedobbo@gmail.com to tomdobson@hotmail.co.uk

Well, I had my doubts, but Mary loves the idea. Much more positive than me in fact. I have to say I'm surprised. From the conversations we've had over the years I got the impression she was dead against dwelling on the past. I know she hates your blog, anyway. As you will read, she is not afraid to write about feelings and relationships. By the way, the girlfriend who told me about the dead guy, was not Mary. I think it was one of her friends called Fay. I would never think of Mary as a girlfriend. As I say, she's the sister we never had. Corny, but true.

Attachment: My prefab memories, by Mary Van der Zee (née Patterson)

Charlie Dobson has asked me to write something about my childhood in a post war prefab, to help his brother Tom's friend Frances with her research project. Charlie has written something, so it's Ok with me, even though I hate books written by people dwelling on the past. I did do history at school, and I liked some of it, but that's not the same as biographies, especially when they are about people nobody has heard of. Ironically, I have been asked to write my own autobiography, on the grounds that I am well known in the science world. I'm still thinking about it.

First, Tom's right, we were like brothers and sister at the beginning. Bill and Agnes loved to tell me about how I always wanted to go next door to play, and, later on, to play out on the Green Thing or up on the hill. I don't think any of us thought about being different, until puberty got in the way. Boys wore underpants and girls wore knickers, and we all knew what was underneath, but that was just how it was. For the record, before my mum got round to the birds and the bees, all the girls knew about sex, so I had to pretend it was a revelation. Anyway, I just wasn't interested. The idea neither fascinated nor revolted me.

I remember our age of innocence as an age of Meccano, Bayco, Dinky toys and getting on top of the Green Thing first. I didn't realise that my mum worried because, in her received wisdom, these were boy's things. Not ladylike. I tried hard to like playing families, dollies and wearing pretty dresses, but only to please mum and dad. What I liked was fighting with the estate boys, but that only made matters worse, and I was grounded several times for that. I feel guilty, even now, about not being a girlie girl; it must have been an embarrassment and a worry for them. I have never managed to talk about my tomboy days with my mum. When I have tried, she always changed the subject. I wonder why.

Reading Charlie's memories, the one I like most was the one about terrorising the little girl on her tricycle. I wish the boys had let me in on the plan. I think I would have been a more plausible bomber.

I always admired Tom, but Charlie and I got on better. Tom was a bit funny about some things, especially as we got older. When their uncle Albert gave the boys his son's discarded fretwork machine, the idea was that they would share it. Tom went headlong for it, but Charlie wasn't interested at all. The first time the saw blade broke, he went off on this roller skates. But I loved watching Tom pedalling way and turning out beautiful art nouveau patterned pipe racks and wooden toys. To start with, Tom would not give me a go, but I managed to get round him one rainy day, and a few burnt out saw blades later, I kind of got the hang of it. After that he let me help him a bit, holding things while the glue set, pasting pictures on for jigsaw puzzles, even cutting when the demand for wooden toys got too much running up to Christmas.

My favourite was a model old fashioned fancy carriage, entirely made out of plywood. Tom used to get the patterns from a magazine called Hobby's Weekly. The fretwork machine was a Hobby's too. Later Tom converted it to run by an electric motor, but it was never quite as good as the old treadle version. This all happened in Tom and Charlie's bedroom, which was not ideal. The sawdust got everywhere, which Olive hated. I loved the smell of it. Once or twice Charlie and I swapped bedrooms so Tom and I could work in peace. Charlie just went next door and slept in my bed. My mum was happy about this because she had had a little boy who died before I was born, but she only told me that years later.

Tom and I should have gone into business really, but he was bad tempered at times. Or got married maybe. The fretwork was fun on rainy days, but like most kids I loved being out, just playing. Climbing trees and lying in the grass on the hill with other kids or paddling in the pond.

I know my mum was very worried about my tomboy ways, as she used to call them, but my dad told me recently that it didn't bother him. Just a phase he said. A phase I'm still in. Tom once told me their Uncle Albert had two women friends who lived together like a married couple. I never met them, but Tom became quite fond of Rose and Jackie. My mum met them too when the three of them came over to see Olive. I think she was afraid I might end up like them. She could not bring herself to utter the word lesbian.

To make mum happy I tried to make friends with girls as well as boys, one or two in the estate days, and more later at my grammar school. I did keep up with some of them until fairly recently. One of them, Maureen, wrote about her prefab experience for me:

'My parents always said just how lucky they had been to be given an 'American style' prefab to live in with the amazing fitted kitchen, we had never heard of such a thing. Cupboards fitted on all walls, a built-in cooker, and a 'copper' to do the washing in and the most amazing thing ... a refrigerator. This fridge was my mother's pride and joy; she had only ever seen one in the 'American movies', and she cleaned it every day.

We had two large bedrooms one for Mum and Dad and the other for us kids. These rooms also had fitted metal wardrobes complete with drawer units and dressing table all built in. Then the fabulous bathroom with its bath complete with taps. We had been using a tin bath that we hung up on a hook outside at my Nan's house in Wembley. There was an airing cupboard all fitted in a very neat way allowing plenty of storage.'

Another friend, Fay, told me:

'The estate was an amazing place to spend the long summer hours of our childhood. I remember a huge area of rolling hills, trees, woods and fields. Many of the fields with cows in them. There was a pond where we used to play. As a child I thought it was massive. We would spend hours fishing in this pond for 'red throats' and other tiddlers using a jam jar with string tied around the top. Summer days just playing in the fields, making endless daisy chains, looking for grasshoppers, climbing trees, walking amongst the cows, never feeling unsafe, only popping home for a slice of bread and jam then out again.'

I must have been somewhere else, I guess.

When I passed the eleven plus, everyone assumed I would go to Canonsbury, but for some reason or other I was selected for a different grammar school, Briscombe High, miles away. Mum thought this was because of my high marks in the exam. I loved the place from the word go. I just loved learning about almost everything, so I prospered. The teachers were mostly friendly, and some of them were quite young, only in their twenties and thirties. The school tried to be like one of the progressive independents. When I heard about some of the things Tom hated at Canonsbury, I realised how lucky I was, and how unfair it was on him.

To please my mum, I also went to Church. I really enjoyed going to the service every Sunday and attending Sunday School in the afternoon. Only a few kids from the prefabs went, so I got to know new friends who lived in town. Sometimes auntie Olive came with us, and Tom started going when his best pal Daniel was the curate's son, but that didn't last long. He must have been about fourteen then. I don't remember Charlie going, and he assures me he was never tempted. Tom and I later discussed religion, whether it was believable and so on, but by then he was an atheist and a socialist. I wasn't sure, but I admired my mother's and Olive's faith. I think it was my mum who converted Olive, probably after she and Harry had gone through a bad patch or something. I know neither Harry nor my dad were convinced. In fact Bill was quite anti, and when he got angry he would criticise mum for her refusal to talk about religion. You could hear everything through those thin walls.

I also picked up something about the church being the reason for the strife between Olive and that welsh woman over road, Mrs Payne. She used to travel miles with her son George and another welsh lady from the prefabs, to go to a chapel. Baptist, I think. I think the other lady's husband used to drive them. Or at least that was what I was told. It was apparently some kind of religious conflict between the Anglicans and the Baptists. Mum told me that Mrs Payne used to bad mouth Olive, calling her a hypocrite because she had not been baptised. I never knew what to make of that George either. Seemed like a sad kind of boy to me. The Dobsons reckoned he used to annoy them to please his mum.

Some of the prefab kids used to take the micky out of me because they had me down as a swot and a snob. My friend Fay wouldn't speak to me for a while, and I overheard mum and dad arguing one day about a woman who had criticised me for liking science and maths. Not subjects for girls, apparently. But Charlie and Tom stuck by me, as did their parents Olive and Harry. Harry especially. I remember him talking to me and Tom about socialism and communism when we were doing our A levels. He didn't have any prejudices against girls doing science, playing football or anything else they fancied. It's all knowledge, he would say. In Russia, women could be engineers or scientists.

I did have a few boyfriends at the grammar school, but I was never in love, not in the lovey-dovey way other girls tried to carry on. Always older boys of course, and usually clever. Just kissing and cuddling. Honestly. We were all terrified of getting pregnant.

I did well in most subjects, and got good reports, but I never showed them to Charlie, who had failed the eleven plus. I thought it might ruin our friendship. Of the two next door I suppose I liked Charlie the best and we still hung out in the holidays. Like when Tom went off with his friend on cycling tours. By this time Charlie was into football, skiffle and cooking, and I caught all those bugs from him.

The skiffle was a laugh. I loved music lessons at school. They taught me to read music and I was in the school choir. Charlie was better than me at learning a tune by ear, and Tom made him a guitar which was always out of tune. Charlie got pretty good at belting out the chords, so we progressed from skiffle to trad jazz, pretending to be in Chris Barber's band. We found a real band in town who had lost their banjo player, but not her banjo. Charlie set to and learned enough chords to get by. He was Lonnie Donegan, and I was Ottilie Patterson. (After all, I had the same surname, and I could sing better than the others.) By the time I was doing my O level mocks, we were getting school gigs and earning peanuts. Literally, usually.

Our shared love of cooking came about because it was the one thing apart from football Charlie loved at school, mainly because he was besotted at the time by an Italian girl, and it was the only way they could be together at school. Chiara already knew how to cook Italian food, and we got on like a house on fire. Her mum used to call me Maria, which made me feel special. The three of us used to cook exotic dishes for both sets of parents, who were always polite about the stuff we served up, even when they hated it. Harry loved it, and he loved having Charlie and his girls in the kitchen.

The prefab idyll ended for me when Charlie joined the Sea Cadets. I tried to join too, but they didn't take girls back then. He dropped the cooking, music, Chiara, and me, to run away to join the merchant navy and see the world. I never really got over it.

I stayed on with my parents, choosing a biology, chemistry and maths A level course at Briscombe. I didn't see much of Tom - we both had holiday jobs and concentrated on our friends at school. I finally left home to study biology at Cambridge. I used to come back to the estate to see Mum and Dad, and I tried to get them to move out, but they always found reasons not to. Once they came over to see me. A few days before they demolished the prefabs. They had just signed up for a new council flat. For the first time in my life I felt homeless

Chapter 26: | Frances' Story

1970 / 2021

Frances Smith thought she had the best mum and dad in the world. When she went to school, one of her classmates asked her why her dad spoke funny. She didn't really understand the question, so when she got home she asked her mum, who told her that her dad spoke with an accent. She explained that people from different places spoke in different ways, according to where they grew up.

'I come from London, so I have a London accent, and so do you because we live in London too.'

'So what accent does dad have then?'

'He has a German accent because he was born in Germany.'

'So am I English or German?'

'You're English because you were born here.'

'But why aren't I half German?'

'Well, I suppose you are really, but it's not a good idea to tell your friends at school just now.'

'Why?'

'Well, before you were born, England and Germany were enemies, and some English people still hate Germans.'

Frances didn't really understand this at the time, but as she grew up she became increasingly aware that having a German father brought her trouble. Although she kept her word, somehow the news had got round about being the daughter of a German called Heinz, so her time at primary school was blighted by bullying. For a start, the other kids used to call her beany, after Heinz baked beans. She even got into a fight with a ginger-headed girl, who called her a Nazi. The boys at school played war games, running around the playground pretending to be RAF pilots shooting down German airmen, or army officers lobbing grenades at German soldiers. To make matters worse, all the films shown at the local cinema seemed to be about how the British or Americans won the war, and the nasty Germans got what they deserved, time after time. Once, on the way home, a boy fired a potato gun at her, yelling take that Fraulein Hitler. For a while, she just put up with it, but one day, just after her eleventh birthday her dad found her sobbing in bed at night.

Mum and dad decided it high time to come clean. They explained that they had met after the war, when dad was a prisoner of war in a camp not so far from where they lived now. His name was then Heinz Schmidt, and he was forced to stay in England to work as a labourer, helping to rebuild houses that had been bombed. They fell in love but dared not tell anyone because it was against the law for German prisoners of war to even talk to English people, but a few years later they changed the law, so Heinz and Angela were married in a church near the PoW camp, and when Heinz was discharged he changed their surname from Schmidt to Smith, in the hope that it would make their life easier.

Frances suspected he had only been told half the story. She decided to shame her tormentors by working hard and outdoing them all.

She was physically strong, and loved all kinds of sport, excelling at athletics, hockey, netball and tennis. She won prizes every year. She was not bad at academic subjects either, getting above average grades in English, French and History. She sailed through the eleven plus, got a bagful of O levels, and joined a tennis club in the sixth form. She never lied about her father's background and always defended her parents. Nobody messed with Frances, and boys adored her.

Through Angela's dogged efforts, the family eventually managed to get on to a council house waiting list, and finally they moved into a terraced house in St. Albans. Over time Heinz's nationality had become less of a problem. He retrained as a draughtsman with a local architecture practice, but his health began to deteriorate after all those years of manual labour and a lifetime of smoking.

When Frances was fourteen, she asked Heinz and Angela to tell her more about their life after the war, before she was born.

They told her how they had been abused and ostracised when people found out that he had fought for Germany. For years he could not find regular work, even though he had studied architecture as a teenager at Hochschule before he was called up. He had to make do with manual labour in the building trade. Even when a decent employer took him on, his co-workers would send him to Coventry or frame him for theft, forcing him on to the dole. He talked about being ashamed that he could not always support her and her mum, who had taken over as the breadwinner, working as a secretary in a factory. For years she chose to keep quiet about the leers and lecherous advances made by men at work, and when Heinz found out she had a hard time persuading him not to make trouble. His sense of shame had never left him.

Frances knew things had been bad but was shocked by the detailed picture they painted. She wondered why they had decided to stay in England. Heinz spelt it out. He no longer had a home in Germany. His own family had been killed in the allied Magdeburg bombing raid, which destroyed most of the town in 1945. Like other PoWs in England, he counted himself lucky; he was treated decently by the British army, a small wage, regular meals, a roof over his head, a few English friends, and the chance to marry the love of his life. Anyway, after the Russian occupation Magdeburg was in the GDR, East Germany, a soviet satellite state, not an attractive option by all accounts.

Once Frances understood the situation, she was still curious about how exactly they had met. Heinz was glad to reminisce. A born storyteller, first he set the scene. Having parachuted from his Junkers 80 bomber and captured somewhere the South of England he was sent to various PoW camps until the armistice in 1945, but he had to stay in England. By 1947 he was stationed at a camp near a town called Rayners Lane, north of London. Every day he and his fellow prisoners would set out on the back of a truck to build new houses and roads for English people. They covered quite a wide area, and they never quite knew which site they would be working on. The site where he met Angela was a prefab estate called Friars Walk. He and his gang were in charge of building the concrete bases on which over a hundred prefabs would be constructed, and the road which would connect them, together with pavements and access paths. The cruel winter of 1946 and 1947 had held up the job, and the future residents were keen to get in, so they were under the cosh. He remembers families who visited during the winter, just to see where they would be living. They were supervised by the English soldiers, who spent most of their time in one of the huts which housed tools and materials.

The PoWs and their guards were on pretty good terms by then, and they used to drink tea and smoke together. In principle, this was forbidden, and they were not supposed to fraternise with residents either, but in practice all kinds of rules were broken, including some black-market deals involving building materials such as sand and cement. Heinz was the gang leader because he was respected by the others and was reliable and spoke the best English. One of the huts was near an electricity distribution box which all the kids called the Green Thing. Heinz used to hide small toys in the sand heap, to give to the kids, when the guard was not around. At first he could not understand why the Green Thing was such an attraction, but one of the boys told him it was a magic box inhabited by little people. The estate kids would hold competitions to prove who could jump on top of the Green Thing and stay up the longest. The PoWs used to bet on them. Being with the estate kids made Heinz happy and sad at the same time. He grieved for his lost family in Magdeburg.

One spring day, a family walked by, including an attractive young lady in a dress with roses on it. He was mixing cement at the time, and she smiled at him. She came by the next day and said hallo. Heinz smiled but pointed to the soldier who was watching. He and put his finger to his lips to indicate he was not able to speak to her. She understood and went on her way, looking back and waving from a safe distance. That was how it started. He didn't see her again for a week or two, but one of the boys who lived in the nearest prefab smuggled a note to him. It was in English, but he understood that her name was Angela, and she was looking after prefab number 52 while her sister and family were away for a fortnight.

'I was so excited Frances. For me it was love at first sight, and I think it was for your mum too. I did a deal with one of the guards. He turned a blind eye for half an hour, in exchange for some cigarettes or something. The rest is history, Frances. Don't worry, you were not conceived until sometime later, when we were allowed time off officially.'

Angela's version of the encounter was slightly different. Yes, she fancied him of course, but her mother, who had noticed the exchange of looks, tried to warn her off, pointing out that the PoWs were strictly out of bounds, blah, blah.

'Typical, my mum. Your grandma Peggy. What a nerve, she wasn't an angel herself. I think she was jealous. I know Sue was. Their attitude only made me determined to see this man again. We just clicked somehow.'

'Have you or mum ever been back to that estate?'

'No, no point. Your auntie Sue and her family went out to Australia in 1957. We fell out when we got married, like the rest of the family. I was shunned because I was sleeping with the enemy. All Germans were Nazis to them. She's dead now anyway. Run over by a tram in Melbourne. I think you have some cousins out there. Boy and a girl, I think.'

'Did many PoWs stay in England?'

'Most were repatriated, but for better or for worse we chose to stay in England, even though my family would have nothing more to do with us.'

'They always called me 'That Nazi', even though I never joined the party. I bear them no ill.'

'Did you kill anyone in the war dad?'

'I suppose our bombs must have killed English people. I have to live with that.'

After both her parents have died, Frances Smith starts researching the story of post war prefabs. She is fascinated by the idea that they were built by German prisoners of war like her father. Could there be anybody who grew up on Friars Walk who might remember her father, the lonely labourer who smuggled toys to English kids?

The keywords she enters in the search engine are prefab Green Thing.

Tom Dobson, now retired and living in Lincolnshire, receives notification of a new comment on his blog. He doesn't recognise the name, Frances Smith, but he checks his list of names anyway. Maybe it's the married name of another girl who lived on the estate. Then he reads the comment.

I think you might remember my father, Heinz Schmidt, who worked as a labourer on Friars Walk prefab estate, when he was a prisoner of war. I believe you may be the one of the children he gave toys to at the electricity box the estate kids called the Green Thing. He stayed in England rather than being repatriated, and he married a lady called Angela he'd met on the estate. I am their daughter, retired from nursing a few years ago, and I have always been interested in finding out more about those days. When my parents died recently I decided to start some research. I know it would be difficult to meet because of the pandemic, but perhaps you could help me track down others who grew up on Friars Walk? I would be glad to hear from anyone else who would be interested in helping me.

For a few moments Tom is back with the prisoner of war at the Green Thing. He thinks about replying on his blog but decides to reply by email.

tomdobson@hotmail.co.uk to *franschmidt@mail.com*

Subject: Your comment

Date: 04/03/21

Thanks for your comment Frances. What a surprise! Of course I remember your father. You might like to know that most people round our corner of the estate felt sorry for him and his comrades and bore them no ill. I would be pleased to help with your research. For a start I can ask my brother Charlie, and Mary, who lived next door to us, for their memories of Friars Walk, and I can ask all those who have commented on this blog if they would like to help you. When things change for the better we could perhaps meet up, but until then, let's keep in touch by email. Best wishes, Tom.

franschmidt@mail.com to tomdobson@hotmail.co.uk

Subject: Your comment

Date: 11/03/21

Hallo again Tom. So glad are up for it.

I forgot to mention that I visited Friars Walk one day in 1970 because I was doing my degree thesis on prefabs, inspired by my father's stories. The only prefabs still standing were yours and your neighbours. Your parents were not in, but I spoke to Mrs Patterson and she said she would pass my request on. Nothing happened though, and in the end I did most of my research on another estate, Pilgrims Way, in Kingsbury. Seems they named estates after religious highways, real or imagined.

A strange thing has happened. I mentioned this to my nephew Matthew, who works for a TV production company. He didn't know anything about post war prefabs, but he's done a bit of googling and he thinks there could be a drama series in this. Something based on your experiences. He would like to talk to you about developing a proposal and pitching to the BBC, ITV or Channel 4. Interested?

Acknowledgements

Friars Walk is imaginary, but I am indebted to those who have so generously allowed me to use their memories of prefabulous life on the estate where my sister and I grew up, Pilgrims Way, London NW9:

Paul Kennedy, Jim and Janet Chignall, Dave Robson, Chrissie Turner, Billy Chambers, Shelagh O'Mahoney, Vic Burton, Wayne Evans, Rob Burns, Alan Newberry

Also, thanks to:

Margaret Dewrance, Madeleine Dewrance, Ben Dewrance, Louise Lamb, Alexandra Heaton, Geoff Thompson, Dave Kenyon, Phil Cosker, Colin and Lys Ann Reiners, Jean Radford, Ivan Sayer, Janet Head, Rhys Jones, Bea Jones, Clare Smith, Philip Grant.

Cover photograph courtesy Jim and Janet Chignall

'The Prefab Museum tells a story that resonates today, of housing shortages – and innovative solutions to them that were enthusiastically embraced by their residents. It also paints a picture of social, domestic, and working class life from 1945 to the present day.

The Prefab Museum was created in March 2014 in a vacant prefab on the Excalibur Estate in south London by Elisabeth Blanchet, photo-journalist, supported by Jane Hearn, community development worker. The museum closed following a fire in October 2014 and since then we have continued to collect and record memories, photographs and memorabilia......'

To find out more online, please visit this excellent resource:

https://www.prefabmuseum.uk/content/about/introducing -website

.

Printed in Great Britain
by Amazon

61613359R00112